Why We Do What We Do

A wise tool for self-understanding. This book identifies our unique 'Inner Family Archetypes' and shows how to skillfully work with these energies to yield deep awareness and wisdom about ourselves and how we relate to others."

–Jan Angel, co-author of *Buddhist Astrology:*
Chart Interpretation from a Buddhist Perspective

An understanding of the inner family archetypes is one of the most practical tools you can have. If you want to transcend human relationships and make responsible personal progress on the path leading to self-mastery, choose now to begin using this book to effect desired change in your life.

–Alberta Fredricksen, retired human resource director, Bozeman Schools

This book is magnificent! It is very well written, easy to read. It is really helpful in understanding your psychology, your relationships and your spiritual path. It is also down to earth and has lots of interesting stories.

–Judy Sue Christenson, RN, Minneapolis, MN

As a former teacher and lawyer, and as a life-long learner I have high standards, and *Why We Do What We Do* rates up there with the best. It has provided some real aha's for both my husband and I in how we interact with each other. I no longer need someone outside me to set boundaries, to listen to me and to help me solve problems, to share my wonder, or to act for me. I can access all of those capacities within so I can have real, authentic, loving relationships with my immediate family and with other people.

–Judy Bouton, reiki master, Beaverton, OR

Why We Do What We Do offers the foundational structure we must understand to effectively heal our bodies, minds, emotions and—most importantly—our souls. This read is a must. It qualifies as one of the top three life-changing events in my life! Blessings.

–Cheryl Laures RN, owner, Whole Body Balancing, Yakama, WA

Learning the unique concepts in this book has infinitely enriched our lives. By understanding the unloving and the loving aspects in ourselves and in others, we have experienced a new world of wholeness.

–Marinus and Martha Jacobs, security officer and office manager, Yakama, WA

This method is a revelation! Finally a way to understand the dynamics of relationships with a map to success!

–Antonia Johnson, wholeness facilitator, Livingston, MT

All the parts of me are explained clearly in *Why We Do What We Do*. In understanding the whole person in myself and in others, life has become so much more enjoyable.

–Robyn Taylor, engineering supervisor, Washington, D.C.

Life-changing concepts! That's what I found in *Why We Do What We Do*. Finally I understand what has been happening in my life and the lives of family, friends and co-workers. This book shows how we are put together and the results of choices that we make. When you understand the choices, you can make better ones for a better life.

–Myriam Ablaza, electrical designer, Los Angeles, CA

I wasn't really living. Then *Why We Do What We Do* came into my world. WOW! What an eye opener! Life is sooo much more enjoyable when you know how to go through it easier. Thanks for giving us this wonderful book!

–Laurie Stewart, researcher, Silver Spring, MD

Why We Do What We Do has been most helpful for me to understand our different personality and behavioral patterns. As a teacher it is absolutely important for us to know this, so we can be authentic with those whom we have the privilege to guide.

–Maria de Lourdes Campos, educator, Quito, Ecuador

I have applied this book to psychotherapy, and found that it helps my clients experience unprecedented empowerment over their lives and circumstances. I recommend this book for exceptionally profound and lasting change.

–Marie Lepeltier, M.A. Psychology, Loveland, CO

A vital and often humorous book. It was immediately one of the most directly useful psychology books that I have ever read. We read it out loud as a family! My 15 year old loves it! I think of it as humorous and spirited "Freud and Jung" for the 21st Century!

–Neil & Linda Kremer, acupuncturists, South Glastonbury, MT

Knowing more of ourselves gives us wider and deeper degrees of freedom and happiness. I highly recommend this book as a road map to self-discovery.

– Marius Michael George, visionary artist and teacher, Pray, MT

Why We Do What We Do has been an invaluable tool for our family. It has helped each one of us understand our own inner dynamics enabling us to interact with greater compassion, appreciation and harmony.

–Cheryl Smith, singer, Emigrant, MT

I gave your wonderful book to many friends, because anyone who wants to understand themselves or others better can benefit from it. Thank you.

– Heather Bjorstadt, mom, Belgrade, MT

I have learned much about myself by reading your book. I have also learned how to better understand my relationship with my husband and other close family members. This has helped me considerably in getting along better with others. Thank you so much.

–Darlinda Stevens-Gibson ESA, Portland, OR

This wisdom book guides you to identify and understand your deepest patterns. It gives you all the skills and tools to make a full transformation from self-sabotage to expressing your highest self in constructive relationships. With its caring guidance, the fine-tuning becomes painless! Don't wait to read it! Every moment of your life is precious!

–Vera K DeLeon, health practitioner, Tigard, OR

The book helps you to understand and deal with your patterns, so you can ultimately get along with others and create healthy adult responses to the uncomfortable situations that we all face in our life.

– Darci Stewart, real estate agent, Bozeman, MT

Archetypes are everywhere, from native studies to Jung psychology. What's great about this book is that it makes archetypes easy to assimilate and to apply to your own psychology.

– Wendy Rawlings, event coordinator, Livingston, MT

This method in this book has helped me tremendously. As a result, I feel that I am in the driving seat of my future.

–Pedro Angel Pinardo, business owner, South Glastonbury, MT

Our ninth and tenth grade students had an adventure in self-discovery reading and discussing together the "four pathways to your authentic self" in our life skills course. The clearly defined principles and the abundant examples from real life and the movies helped to anchor the concepts and spark discussion. A great life text!

–M. Lombard, Principal, Longfellow Academy, North Glastonbury, MT

Wow. It's so clear. It's so easy to read. It fits like a puzzle. I've been putting it to the test with myself, my family and now my clients. By applying the new wisdom that jumps out at you from each page, your compassion for others will increase one hundred fold. It will permeate your world and bless others. You really will understand why people do what they do. For myself, I have stopped the self-criticism. I appreciate myself more. Can you imagine what a relief that is? This book promotes love, love within—where it really counts

– Molly A. Valerio, psychotherapist LCSW, BCD, Indianapolis, IN

Why We Do What We Do provides a different view of psychology and lets us take a peek at ourselves in a new way. I have benefited a lot from the book and strongly recommend it to people who want to know more about the Self.

–Yin Ming Lee, aerospace engineer and independent business owner, Butte, MT

This book gave me healing and brought me to a new level of consciousness. The teaching in it helped me to find my true identity, heal my pain, regain my inner peace and find the love of my life. Thank you.

–Julie Galienne, project manager, Ottawa, Canada

This reader-friendly book is an essential handbook for anyone actively involved in self-transformation. It accurately describes the language of the soul. After reading *Why We Do What We Do*, you learn what to do about it!

–Kathie Garcia, transformational astrologer, Emigrant, MT

This book is an invaluable gift for improving communication skills. It played a key role in saving and improving our marriage when others were choosing divorce. Thanks to this book, the art of getting along with others has just gotten so much easier. It should be required reading in every college.

–Daniel and Valery O'Connell, information specialists Pray, MT

This work has taught me much about my psychology, and resulted in the following benefits: more positive interpersonal relationships, less difficult "difficult" people, and more successful work projects! I strongly recommend this book to anyone who is seeking to improve their life.

–David Shipley Alexander, senior engineer, NASA projects, Butte, MT

I am particularly grateful for the knowledge I acquired through this work to understand my conscious thinking and subconscious reaction patterns. This has affected positive change in my personal and business relationships.

–Orlando Johnson, retired corporate economist, South Glastonbury, MT

This teaching helps us release our most private shame and grievous losses, which are hidden on the other side of our awareness. By understanding this teaching, I have restored to me some of my most longed for parts, and my most tiresome complexities cleaved like a psychological Gordon knot.

–Charles McDonald, sales representative, Bozeman, MT

This book is the key to resolve and transcend those aspects in my psyche, which were stopping me from making progress. When I finished translating the book into Spanish, I wasn't the same person. I felt better about myself, and my relationships with others. I still have a lot to learn from the book, but, at least, I am beginning to know why I do what I do.

–Juan Lidon Asensio, English professor, Orihuela, Spain

This work has helped me get to what I have danced around for years. Facing myself, rather than looking at and blaming others, has been a most difficult but rewarding growth process.

–Cheryl Upshaw, Emigrant MT

The difference between this and other methods is that it lifts you right out of the problem into an understanding that is so very comforting. It is so empowering to see the drama outside and inside of you and to realize that now, you are becoming the director of your own life.

–Mary Cummins, receptionist, Denver, CO

Working with the inner family archetypes has been a joyous experience of self-revelation. I have found this approach to be liberating to my soul as well as healing to my mind and my body.

–Yvonne Buck, occupational therapist, Aurora, CO

The inner family model helped us to better understand how each person on our work team thinks and feels. This generated more good will in our office and helped us to accomplish more together.

–George Makris, VP marketing, Bozeman, MT

Working with your inner family is one of the best things you can do for yourself. It helps me heal my soul and guides me in the process of understanding how my psyche inhibits or assists me on my spiritual path.

–Elizabeth Hoyt, licensed clinical social worker, Lakewood, CO

This enlightened approach to healing our psyche. The techniques of this model helped me understand where I am at any given moment so I am empowered to choose a higher, more loving way. This has done wonders for my interpersonal relationships and helped me to bond with my beautiful soul.

–Lucy AM Crown, retired police officer, Montreal, Canada

Knowing the dynamics of our inner family explained in this book sets the stage for the development of a healthy outer family.

–Martin Hildreth, ornamental blacksmith and father of four boys, Emigrant, MT

My husband, family, and I first worked with the inner family archetypes over ten years ago, and we have been using it ever since. I have also used the model professionally for the last four years in both individual and group counseling. I feel my clients have benefited from applying the model to many types of problems, including depression, abuse, relationships with family members, and lack of self-esteem.

–Marilynne Lambert, mental health therapist, Bonnyville, AB, Canada

Working with the family archetypes turned my life around at a critical time. It is simply amazing to experience the change and ensuing joy that has occurred in myself and in my family through a classic watershed effect since working with these concepts. Thanks Brian, Caroline and Therese.

–Deanna Campbell, corporate trainer, Bozeman, MT

Understanding the principles that underlie everything I think, say, and do has been the source of my freedom. Today, people comment on my smiling, laughing, and pleasant outlook on life. It is such a relief to have the weights lifted off my shoulders and the sunshine on my face. I look forward to the rewards of infinite successes the rest of my life.

–Katherine Thomas, engineer, Salt Lake City, UT

By applying the inner family archetypes in the classroom and at home, I found that I can optimally help children develop their full potential.

–Alethea Lambert, Montessori teacher, Bozeman, MT

Working with the family archetypes is easy and very efficient, and the results are immediate. When I don't feel good, I use the dialogue technique, and almost instantaneously I feel better. When I anticipate some challenging situations, I make sure that all my family archetypes are functioning in perfect harmony, by using affirmations or a dialogue. It is simple and it works! I am happier than I have ever been.

–Celine Delbeque, immigration project leader, Montreal, Canada

The inner family archetype model opened our eyes to the network of psychological forces underlying human relationships and transformed us. We had been working on my psychology for more than a decade, but nothing had near the impact that the inner family archetype therapy had on us. We now understand how to overcome insecurities and achieve a greater sense of wholeness and inner strength.

–Daniel and Sylvie Wildgen, builder and learning specialist, Ottawa, Canada

Having studied a number of psychological models, I have found none match the power of the inner family archetypes. These archetypes are an invaluable tool in sensitive communication processes with family, friends and colleagues. I am much more likely now to be effective with others, and much less likely to cause misunderstanding. My life would lack its present richness without this awareness. Assimilating the inner family archetypes has helped me understand the underlying forces that influence the people I meet, and has given me a greater capacity for patience and good will towards all.

–Lynne Monds, public relations consultant, Santa Monica, CA

The inner family archetypes are a gift from God. Studying them in others and myself has been a life-changing event. By understanding them, I made the first baby steps towards greater wholeness. If you have a hard time coming to grips with the concept of healing your inner child, this system will give you practical tools to change for the better. Not only will you be rewarded, but others around you will be uplifted as well.

–Rudy Parker, sales associate, Bozeman, MT

WHY WE DO
WHAT WE DO

FOUR PATHWAYS
TO YOUR AUTHENTIC SELF

Caroline Hanstke
Brian Emmanuel Grey
Therese Emmanuel Grey

2004
Sirius Publishing Partners

WHY WE DO WHAT WE DO: *Four Pathways to Your Authentic Self*
By Caroline Hanstke, Brian Emmanuel Grey and Therese Emmanuel Grey

First Edition
First Printing, 2004

Cover design by Janice Booker-Benight

Note to the reader: All of the case studies in this book are real, but the names and some of the circumstances have been changed to protect our clients' anonymity. The archetypal assessments of celebrities included in this book are based on their public—not their private—life. They illustrate an archetypal pattern of behavior and are not intended to limit anyone.

Printed in the United States of America

Dedication

We dedicate this book to the great lights
of East and West who have inspired us
and left footprints in the sand
for us to follow.

In Gratitude

We wish to thank all of our inner teachers, clients, friends and loved ones who have stood by us year after year, and helped us bring forth this work. We wish to honor the people who have helped us produce this book—Patricia Spadaro-Yorwerth and Marie Lepeltier for their assistance in editing; Virginia Wood for her assistance in transcribing and proofing; Rudy Parker and John Paul and Jeanette Mathis for their assistance in graphic design; and Nigel Yorwerth, George Makris, and Deanna Campbell for their sales and marketing guidance. We also extend a special thank you to Orlando and Antonia Johnson for going the extra mile to support us in every possible way. May you be blessed many times over for your giving hearts.

TABLE OF CONTENTS

Foreword

by Helen Collier

For many years, I have trained people in the United States and around the world on how to increase self-esteem, develop will power, and achieve their material and spiritual goals by nurturing the body, the mind, and the soul in an integrated way. Together with my late husband Bob, who studied directly with Napoleon Hill, I was led to many pioneers in the fields of physical, psychological, and spiritual healing, and the science of mind.

In the early nineties, I came across the teachings on the inner family archetypes brought forth by Caroline Hanstke, and Brian and Therese Emmanuel-Grey. Like other pioneers before them, these authors break the mold with the past. They offer an understanding of self that is original, unique, and powerful, based on four archetypes that are an intrinsic part of our core self, and that encompass all of the positive and negative attitudes found in human nature.

Using the symbols of the Father, the Mother, the Boychild, and the Girlchild, each archetype that Caroline, Brian, and Therese introduce is simple and easy to relate to. It represents a specific role that we play at one point or another in life. When we understand these roles, we see our strengths and weaknesses in a new light. We learn to correct negative behavior that does not represent who we really are nor who we are meant to be. We begin to honor and appreciate both our masculine and feminine sides.

The beauty of this system is that it also correlates with four levels of self where each archetype functions—the spirit or superconscious level, the mind or conscious level, the emotions or subconscious level, and the physical body or unconscious level. As my own students studied each level of self, they started to see how their pattern of personal archetypes had affected their behavior and their relationships, for better or worse.

Since the early nineties, I personally got to know Caroline, Brian, and Therese and was able to recognize the gifts that each one brings to this work. Brian's creativity soars as he taps into Infinite Intelligence. Like many geniuses before him, he can access the wisdom of his superconscious to bring forth ideas that help move civilization forward. What Brian teaches cannot be found in a book. It comes from the higher mind and converts people by the very nature of its truth. Caroline, who is a practicing psychologist, works with Brian as a team, applying and expanding these concepts in clinical, corporate, and counseling settings. Caroline has also learned to master the expression of her four loving archetypes. Her sincerity touches the hearts of those who contact her. Therese first came into contact with Brian and Caroline as a client, diligently pursuing her journey for personal wholeness. She brings her dedication to this work and the communication skills needed to see it reach more and more people.

As you explore this teaching, let yourself to be moved. Be willing to stretch your limits. Allow yourself to reconnect with parts of you that may have been dormant or neglected. By doing so, you will experience a new level of unfolding that will enrich your life. Caroline, Brian, and Therese will show you a path of self-discovery that fullfills the ancient adage: "Man, know thyself," so you too, can live life to the fullest.

Why We Do What We Do

In their work with individuals, families and businesses, psychologist Caroline Hanstke and intuitive Brian Emmanuel Grey identified four principles that can teach you to love authentically, powerfully and safely, so you can strengthen your relationships and accomplish your life's purpose. These four principles are:

1. Drawing your boundaries.
2. Embracing your inner teacher.
3. Discovering what drives you.
4. Appreciating your muse.

Each principle relates to one of four specific archetypes imbedded in everyone's consciousness—the inner Father, the inner Mother, the inner Boychild and the inner Girlchild. Archetypes are like pictures—worth a thousand words. They wrap up hundreds of ideas, feelings and impressions into one concept. The archetypes Caroline, Brian and Therese work with are snapshots of our psyche. They gives us important clues as to why we do what we do and what it will take for us to become more authentic with ourselves and with others.

Over the years, Caroline and Brian have used the four principles and their corresponding archetypes to coach individuals and groups on their quest for self-mastery, to heal relationship problems and to mediate human resource issues in large and small business organizations. Using the principles and the tools shared in this book, Caroline and Brian's clients have experienced profound, positive changes in their lives and relationships.

Your inner family archetypes are very powerful. No matter what your gender, your inner Father, inner Mother, inner Boychild and inner Girlchild affect the way you relate to others and the way other people see you. They influence how you think and feel, what you like and dislike and what you aspire to.

Each archetype can be expressed in a loving and unloving way. When you choose the loving behavior, you become authentic. You are your best self. You expand your competencies and you enjoy healthy interactions with others. You feel empowered to give your greatest gifts to life. When you yield to negative archetypal behavior, you sabotage your opportunity to truly be authentic and you undermine your life and your relationships.

To work with your four archetypes—Father, Mother, Boychild and Girlchild—you must first understand how they function through you, with their positive and negative traits. You will discover five fundamental steps to self-knowledge.

The first step is to become aware of your spiritual connection through your superconscious mind. This spiritual connection is influenced by the archetype you aspire to most. The second step is to recognize your specific thinking style, that plays out through your conscious mind and through the archetype you reason with. The third step is to tap your emotions deep in your subconscious mind. These emotions are colored by the archetype you feel through. The fourth step is to discover the sabotaging mechanism in your unconscious mind and its corresponding archetype, so you can make it work for you instead of against you. The fifth step is identifying your social mask, the image you were trained to relate through, and the archetype it expresses.

The more you work with these steps, the more you will begin to see the specific archetypal pattern you printed that is yours to master. This will help you to understand in a new and most profound way why you do what you do. By observing your strengths and weaknesses with equanimity and replacing negative, inherited behaviors with more effective and loving alternatives, you will better appreciate yourself and your loved ones and create mutually rewarding relationships that will enrich your life.

PART ONE

FOUR PRINCIPLES THAT MAKE YOU AUTHENTIC

One

Draw Your Boundaries

To thine own self be true,
and it must follow, as the night the day,
thou canst not then be false to any man.
—William Shakespeare

No matter how the Father figure you grew up with behaved, there is a Loving Father inside of you that will help you draw boundaries and bring order, protection and direction to your life. This Loving Father archetype will help you to be authentic in your interactions with others. It will help you to be reliable and true to your word. It will help you to be firm, emphatic and fair.

The Loving Father always inspires us to take the high road. With him, we experience conditional love that lays down the law. Like the parent who tells the child, "Do not touch the hot iron or you will get burnt," the Loving Father tells us, "Just because what you're doing right now will not have a ramification for two weeks or a month or a year, I'm going to tell you the ramification now. If you eat too much chocolate, you're going to get sick. If you cheat on your wife, she'll eventually find out. If you lie, you're going to feel terrible, even if you do not get caught."

The Loving Father is just. He has our best interests at heart. He allows for our mistakes, but he requires us to learn from them. He disciplines us to protect us. Like parents who remind their child that doing a bad thing does not make him a bad person, the Loving Father corrects our wrong actions without condemning us. He also makes it so that other people can no longer walk all over us. He sets the standards in our relationships and commands respect.

Jared, who worked as a painting contractor, was having a very difficult time on the job. The people with whom he was contracting took advantage of him again and again. They refused to pay him his worth and intimidated him into taking less than his fair share. Jared had learned about the inner family archetypes. He could see that he needed more of the Loving Father to strengthen his personal boundaries and command respect from others. He started using affirmations to engage his Loving Father archetype and practiced saying, "I AM my Loving Father, protecting, directing and disciplining me," every day when he was alone.

At the beginning, Jared had trouble convincing himself it was really going to work. Then, he got the idea of saying it in his head whenever a new contractor tried to pay him less than his due. He would look that person in the eye and think to himself, "I AM my Loving Father conditionally loving my loved self and I am worthy of right compensation for my efforts." He started choosing people who represented good role models of Loving Father to him and visualized their presence over him while he was doing this.

Jared's affirmations became a part of his internal self-talk, and his self-worth improved. Next thing you know, he was able to speak up for himself. As Jared's Loving Father came on line, other people sensed it and started treating him with respect. Eventually, Jared even found he had more work than he could handle, and his financial situation dramatically improved.

The Loving Father makes it so that we can stand, face and conquer personal problems and challenging situations. He also helps us to be more impersonal to affronts, so we stop taking offense. Louis was working with a business contact who challenged his authority as head of the company. The person was used to being the "big fish" and to having everyone knuckle under and cower in his presence. To stay on top of the situation, Louis had to dig in and become the Loving Father, even though he felt nervous about it. He became impersonal to the affront and addressed his contact with an attitude of fairness, integrity and non-compromise. The person backed down, stunned that Louis did not respond personally, emotionally and aggressively to his bully tactics. He said someone had given him wrong information and that it was just a misunderstanding.

When our Loving Father speaks through us, he uses the word "<u>you.</u>" "You" is a very powerful word. Whenever we think of the power word "you," followed by a loving statement or direction, such as, "<u>You</u> need to go and do this," or "<u>You</u> did well," our Loving Father archetype is speaking to us.

The wizard Gandalf, in the 2001 motion picture *Lord of the Rings: The Fellowship of the Ring*, is a good example of the Loving Father. When Gandalf is confronted with the demon Balrog, Gandalf summons his faith in the powers of light, stretches forth his staff and gives a Loving Father decree: "I'm the servant of the secret fire, wielder of the flame of Anor. The dark fire will not avail you! Flame of Udun! Go back to the shadow! YOU... SHALL... NOT... PASS!!!" As Gandalf slams his staff, a flash of white light drives the Balrog back and drops him into a chasm of oblivion.

When we use the word "you" emphatically, backed by the Loving Father's direction, a lot of power flows through us, which can sometimes make other people uncomfortable. Still, it is important to practice the Loving Father's presence in our interactions with others.

With the Loving Father, we have the wherewithal to function effectively in life. We have the strength that we need to make things happen and the perseverance to finish what we start. We also have the proper vision of what we must accomplish, because he gives us a blueprint to follow and provides the right matrix that will lead us to success.

Accessing the Loving Father's protection, direction and discipline can be challenging because there is an Unloving Father archetype within us that seeks to usurp him. This archetype is our inner critic. When we yield to it, we dismantle the Loving Father's circle of protection.

Unloving Father sabotages our ability to draw healthy boundaries by eroding our self-esteem. He criticizes our every move under the guise of looking out for us. He is a tyrant who misuses his power. He controls us by condemning us. He is ruthless, rigid, intimidating, shaming, scornful, and cynical. He is inconsistent, unreliable and arbitrary and can only be counted on to be malefic.

Unloving Father also uses the word "you", but it is always negative. Whenever we catch ourselves thinking, "You're incompetent, you'll never measure up, you're worthless, there's something wrong with you," Unloving Father is operating inside of us.

With Unloving Father, we are besieged by self-criticism. We are controlled by negative motivation, where the basic message we tell ourselves is, "Do it or else!" How many people get out of bed and say, "Hello world, I love you! I cannot wait to start my work and I'm going to be happy"? It is likely that more people get up with Unloving Father saying something like, "You idiot! Hurry up, you're going to be late. Look at what a mess you are. You're going to go out looking like that?" We can never be good enough for Unloving Father. He devastates us by taking away our self-confidence and self-esteem. He knows where we are most vulnerable. What he says to us always has a small kernel of truth that is blown out of proportion but that convinces us of his righteousness.

When we criticize ourselves, other people can sense it. This encourages them to criticize and abuse us too. When they do, we must remember that they are only effective, because they reinforce our internal criticism patterns. If it were not for our own Unloving Father program, they would not get to us.

Our self-criticism also pushes us to criticize others. We build an accumulation of inferiority through these accumulated experiences of self-criticism and often seek to discharge them through a superiority mechanism. Unloving Father tells us we're no good—but far superior to the guy next door. He gets us to find someone worse off than we are, so we can feel superior. This critical projection pacifies him for a short while and gives us a sense of reprieve.

The irony is that when people consciously think they are superior to others, it is often because of a subconscious sense of inferiority. Their overt dominance is an attempt to hide their secret subconscious vulnerability. The reverse is also true. People who consciously think they are inferior usually feel superior subconsciously. They may appear to be everybody's doormat, but they secretly feel that they are better than those who tread upon them. Either way, it is a lose-lose situation validated by Unloving Father.

Our Father archetype is often scrambled, with loving and unloving attributes mixed together. This makes it hard to discern whether a relationship is truly loving or unloving. We may balk at Loving Father relationships that facilitate our growth, because we think other people are unloving when they are only trying to protect us. We may also defend negative Unloving Father relationship patterns, because we convince ourselves that abusive criticism is constructive and deserved.

Until we fully exercise our Loving Father archetype internally, we can function with the help of an "alpha grid." Alpha grids can be likened to the code of chivalry that kept the knights in shining armor fighting within a set of parameters. They are a set of boundaries that we create or accept from outside of ourselves. They protect us and help run our lives smoothly and can be a very powerful focus of the Loving Father in our lives. Some alpha grids are established by society, like traffic laws. Other alpha grids are internal guidelines we may have absorbed from our family or socialization training. Either way, alpha grids only work to the extent that everyone agrees to obey the rules set up within the grid.

While Caroline and Brian worked for an oil company's human resources department, Sharon shot right up the corporate ladder by giving powerful workshops and seminars. The CEO secretly sat in on some of her workshops and before long, promoted her into the vice-president work group and gave her a substantial increase in pay. Sharon was the most talked about "wonder woman" in the company's culture.

Shortly thereafter, she came into the Human Resources office and burst into tears. "I'm an idiot!" she said. "I don't know anything. What am I doing?"

Sharon explained that she had just come from a vice-president meeting where one of the vice presidents leaned across the table and said with great aggression, "What do you do here, anyway?" From the look on the faces around the table, she saw they resented that someone who was not a vice president had an equal vote.

"What happened?" she asked. Caroline and Brian explained that she had lost her alpha grid. They asked her to compare the VP work group with her job as a workshop facilitator, where she was praised. They asked her to describe exactly what would happen when she gave a workshop. Sharon told them, "As I'm walking to the convention center or wherever the lecture is to be, I let my mind relax and I see the people welcoming me. When I arrive, the people are always sitting quietly chatting with their neighbor, waiting. I step up to the lectern, looking down to organize my notes. By the time I look up, the whole room is in silence and I launch into my lecture."

They explained that what made her audience behave was an alpha grid, a set of implicit rules stating that when the lecturer stands at the lectern, the group must be silent and receptive. They said, "The lecture format supplies you with an alpha grid of protection that makes up for your lack of the Loving Father."

"So my ability to unfold my creative nature is the result of a clear set of rules that everyone must follow?" Sharon asked.

"Yes," they replied, "an impersonal code of conduct that all must follow. This is the Loving Father. When your Loving Father archetype is not developed within you, it must be supplied from an alpha grid outside of yourself, and you are vulnerable in situations where there is no grid."

Sharon realized that when she went into the vice-president meetings, no one waited for her to speak, because the lecture alpha grid did not apply there. Seeing her as an inferior, the VPs sniffed out where she was critical of herself and reflected her Unloving Father back to her. Without the Loving Father's protection supplied internally or externally, her creativity did not flow, and she could not receive the approval she was seeking. She came to realize how important it was to internalize the Loving Father, so she would no longer be dependent on an external set of rules and at the whim of those who do not respect them.

It is important to get used to our Loving Father archetype, to enforce the boundaries he sets for us and to feel comfortable with them. Otherwise, Unloving Father's criticism will continue to drown out the voice of the Loving Father and prevent us from experiencing the protection and direction we need to build healthy relationships. With the Loving Father, we stop criticizing ourselves and reacting to the judgments other people send that reinforce how we condemn ourselves. We do not let outside opinions define who we are. We take accountability for our actions; we take responsibility for how other people relate to us, and we take charge of our life.

Tools to Engage Your Loving Father

1. *Ask yourself these questions.*

The following questions can help you assess the Loving Father's presence in your life:

Do you set loving and firm boundaries for yourself?
Do you appropriately protect yourself and others?
Do you set your own standards of behavior?
Do you keep your word, your promises?
Do you tell yourself when you have done a good job?
Do you tell yourself you will learn from your mistakes?
Are you fair?
Are you proactive?
Are you powerful, strong, firm and focused?
Do you honor the law of cause and effect?
Do you see discipline as a protection, rather than a punishment?
Do you function efficiently and productively?
Do you finish what you start?

If you answered yes to most of these questions, your Loving Father is active in your life. If you could not answer "yes," use the tools below to expand his presence in your life and overcome Unloving Father momentums.

2. *Find a role model.*

Watch for examples of the Loving Father in your daily experience, in motion pictures or in stories. Sir

Thomas More in the 1966 motion picture *A Man for All Seasons,* starring Paul Scofield, is an example of the Loving Father in action, who never compromises his principles and upholds the law regardless of the consequences.

3. Set your boundaries.

You can increase your self-confidence by setting boundaries for yourself and honoring them. Stand by your convictions. Notice whether you can calmly correct someone who transgresses your boundaries, without putting them down.

4. Practice impersonality.

Become impersonal when other people try to push your buttons. Find a situation in your past that was difficult for you, when you did not react from your gut or counter-attack. Ask yourself, "How was it that I had the ability to be impersonal, to be detached enough not to let others' criticism stick to me?" Use this insight to do it again, when another opportunity to be impersonal comes into your life.

5. Stop criticizing yourself and others.

When you criticize yourself, and when you allow other people to criticize you, you become negatively defined. You do not honor the boundaries your Loving Father sets for you. Remember that other people can only get to you if their opinion triggers your own Unloving Father. Are you defensive about feedback from others? Are you uncomfortable with authority figures? These are signs of Unloving Father in your life.

Once you know how your Unloving Father manifests himself, claim your Loving Father to replace him.

6. Pay attention to your internal dialogue.

The Father archetype always communicates with the word <u>you</u>. When you catch yourself saying to yourself, "<u>You</u> this," or "<u>You</u> that," notice whether the message is loving or unloving. Then, start practicing more loving self-talk after the word you, like "<u>You</u> did good job. <u>You</u> are a good person. <u>You</u> do not need to let other people trespass your boundaries."

7. Give Loving Father affirmations.

The following affirmations can help you anchor the presence of the Loving Father:

I AM my Loving Father.
I AM protecting and directing my life.
I AM disciplining myself.
I AM setting loving boundaries for myself and others.
I AM in charge of my destiny.
I AM not moved by circumstances and by other people.
I AM inner strength.
I AM honoring Mother.
I AM protecting and directing my Girlchild and my Boychild.

Two

Embrace Your Inner Teacher

You cannot teach a man anything.
You can only help him find it within himself.
—Galileo

Inside each of us is an inner teacher that nurtures and guides us through life, and helps us to be authentic. This inner teacher is the presence of our Loving Mother archetype.

Whether or not our needs for mothering were met in childhood, we can connect with our inner Loving Mother who brings warmth and nurturance to encourage us on our way. She gives us the intimacy that exists between a mother and her child and she helps us to be intimate with others. In every situation, she provides the healing unguent of wisdom and unconditional love that soothes our distress. Like poet, Kahlil Gibran, described, "The mother is everything in life. She is the consolation in our sadness, the hope in our distress, the strength in our weakness.*"

The Loving Mother also draws out the best in us and helps us to succeed. When Caroline was doing her post-graduate work at New York University, her supervisor, Lloyd Silverman, who was a very creative researcher, introduced her to a study he was

---

* Kahlil Gibran. *The Prophet.* New York, N.Y.: Knopf Publishing. 2000

conducting with two other psychologists. Through their research, Silverman and his colleagues had discovered that when women were exposed to the subliminal message, "Mommy and I are one," they were able to lose more weight than those who did not receive that message. When disturbed adolescents were exposed to the message "Mommy and I are one," they improved their reading test scores up to four times more than those who did not receive the message. When smokers who tried giving up cigarettes were checked after a month, 67 percent of those who had been exposed to that message were able to abstain, versus 12.5 percent for those who had not. *

The Loving Mother tells us where we stand. She explains why the Loving Father's discipline, direction and protection are good for us. She backs his disciplines and conditional love with unconditional love and explanation.

Therese often experienced this when her daughter was a toddler. When she would misbehave, Therese's Loving Father archetype would come out with his boundaries and discipline. "You're going to your room," she would say, "and you will only come out when you can stop fussing and change your attitude." Once her daughter calmed down and could reason again, Therese allowed her Loving Mother to step in, taking special time to comfort her child and explaining why she was given a time-out.

People who speak through the Loving Mother are less likely to experience a communication breakdown in their relationships, because the people they relate to feel validated, accepted and included. The Loving

---

* Silverman, Lloyd; Lachmann, Frank; Milich, Robert. *The Search for Oneness*. New York, N.Y.: International Universities Press, Inc, 1982.

Mother explains the "who, what, where, when and why" of every situation. Whenever we say something like, "George (who) was upset (what) at work (where) yesterday (when) because his shipment didn't arrive (why)," our Loving Mother archetype is speaking. We are thorough and we cover all the bases.

The Loving Mother is inclusive. "It is <u>our</u> problem, <u>we</u>'re going to solve it, it is up to <u>us</u>," she says, using the dialogue words "<u>we, our, us</u>." She stands at our side to bring out the best in ourselves and in other people. She helps us to relate sincerely. When we engage her in earnest, the most incredible changes can take place.

After six months of Inner Family work, Brian's client Tamara said to him, "Just show me how you do this mental karate, because usually, within a couple of weeks, I can take a person down. So teach me that and forget about this lovey-dovey crap."

"There's no mental karate going on," Brian said. "I'm just working through the "who, what where, when and why" with earnestness."

Later, Tamara confessed: "When I originally came to see you, I really only came to debunk you. But the other day, I ran into someone I hadn't seen for a long time. 'Excuse me,' she said, 'I do not mean to bother you, but I've noticed such an incredible change in you. Before, I was so scared of you that I would not even ask you a question. But now you seem approachable. What have you been doing?'"

"'Well,' I told her defensively, 'I've been doing some work on myself. Is there anything wrong with that?' She didn't know what to say. I thought about it afterwards and for the first time, I felt like a good person. I realized I had changed, even in spite of myself."

The Loving Mother loves us unconditionally. She helps us to find and nurture the goodness in ourselves and in others, so it can expand. She can work miracles in our lives by holding the immaculate concept for us. She tells us, "You are your best self," and steadily holds that vision for us until we succeed.

Beth was a devout lady in her sixties who had a psychological breakdown and was on heavy medication. Beth's psychiatrist had worked with her for years. One day she told him that she had decided to get additional coaching and that with his help, Brian's help, God's help, and the help of other counselors, she would be all right. This wise doctor honored her resolve and offered to share her case history with Brian and with the counselors with whom she had chosen to work.

Brian's plan was simple—to give Beth the Loving Mother she had never received in her life, to validate her goodness and the great effort she put forth every day to make the world a better place. For six months, he talked to Beth every night on the phone before she went to bed. He would read or tell her stories that, in one way or another, always addressed her enormous devotion to God.

Slowly but surely, Beth got better. At first, she checked in with her psychiatrist every week, then every other week and finally once a month. During an interview six months later, her doctor was stunned. "I do not know what happened to you," he said, "but you're a completely different person." Holding the highest vision for ourselves and for others is the most powerful way to improve our lives and impact our relationships. That is what the Loving Mother teaches.

Embracing the wisdom of our Loving Mother archetype is not always easy, especially if Unloving Mother shows up first. Unloving Mother is the archetypal pattern that supplants our inner teacher. It offers an easy way out.

Unloving Mother does not personally give of herself or go the extra mile. Instead, she offers to spoil us and abandons us along the way. Like a pied piper, she hints that she will satisfy our longings, and she entices us to chase after her, to our own demise. Her behavior breaks down into two tracks—aloof and smother-mother.

Aloof mother abandons people in their moment of need, like a baby on the doorstep. She says, "I have what you want, but I will not give it to you until I get what I want. I'll ignore you until I get my way. I do not care. You're on your own. Your needs are not important to me. Do not make any demands on me because I will not respond to them."

Smother-mother manipulates through flattery. She always gives something in place of herself. She gushes sympathetically, but what she is really saying is, "I do not care enough about you to really give myself personally to you." When the little boy comes along asking for a hug, she gives him some candy and tells him to go play in the yard. By the time the child is a teenager, this pattern balloons. He has figured out that by putting pressure for intimacy on the parent who has a smother-mother mechanism, he can get video games, mountain bikes or cars.

Susan had a smother-mother tendency. She confessed to Caroline and Brian, "I do not know what's going on with my fourteen-year-old daughter. She knows just how to punch my buttons all the time.

She knows how to make me feel guilty so she can get whatever she wants." Susan had been training her daughter from infancy to give her guilt trips so she could then give her something to placate her wants. The daughter figured out early on that if Mommy was not going to give of herself, she would really have to pay, and at fourteen, even asked for a motorcycle. With the help of counseling, Susan learned to be authentic with her daughter and to give her the nurturing she needed, and the situation dramatically improved.

Unloving Father's criticism is hard to bear, but the flip-flop between Loving and Unloving Mother can be even more devastating. One moment, we experience unconditional love with someone who nurtures, teaches and guides us. The next moment, the person becomes artificial or even stone cold, not seeming to care whether we live or die. The polarization between the two leaves us feeling painfully and completely betrayed.

In some hunter-gatherer societies, capital punishment was supplanted by an Unloving Mother punishment, which they believed was worse than death. When someone was in extreme breach of their tribal or spiritual laws, they were turned into a "ghost." No one could offer them food or shelter or even the most rudimentary acknowledgment. Other tribal members were no longer allowed to look at them or talk to them. Those who did became "witches" and were also turned into ghosts. This form of abandonment was so intense that eventually, the castaways lost their minds and did not even bother wearing clothing. They devolved into the wraithlike figures that the collective consciousness of the tribe had commanded.

The world is hungry for the Loving Mother. Everybody longs for her—for the incredible touch, the depth of feeling, the intimacy and the earnestness they received, or should have received, as children. We pursue unconditional love in every relationship we get into and would barter everything we have to get it, when all we have to do is awaken our own inner teacher.

The more we develop our Loving Mother archetype, the less likely we are to fall into codependent relationships. Nurtured by our inner teacher, we do not have to rely on others to feel whole. We can focus on giving and receiving in appropriate ways. We can go the extra mile when that is what is called for, and we do not feel spent. We can also love selflessly, because our needs have been met, and because we know that "the mother's love is not given to us to spoil us with indulgence, but to soften our hearts, that we may in turn soften others with kindness.*"

---

* Paramahansa Yogananda, *Inner Reflections 2000.* Self Realization Fellowship, 2000.

Tools to Engage Your Loving Mother

1. Ask yourself these questions.

The following questions can help you assess the Loving Mother's presence in your life:

Are you warm and personal?
Are you nurturing and caring?
Do you encourage and support yourself and others?
Do you give counsel to others when they need it?
Can you love people no matter what mistakes they make?
Are you available when you are needed?
Do you recognize gifts and talents, be they yours or others?
Do you help yourself and others deal with pain?
Do you respect independence for yourself and your loved ones?
Do you nurture those who are ailing?

If you answered yes to most of these questions, your Loving Mother is very present in your life. If not, use the tools below to expand her presence and overcome Unloving Mother tendencies.

2. Contact your inner teacher.

When things perplex you or trouble you, try and go within to find the answers, instead of relying on outside sources. Listen to the still, small voice inside your heart that teaches you through the presence of the Loving Mother. The insights you receive will be tailored just for you, to help you where you need it most.

3. Nurture life.

To develop the Loving Mother, find ways to nurture life, to teach people and to love them, like Mother Teresa said, even "until it hurts." There are several good documentaries of Mother Teresa that demonstrate the qualities of the Loving Mother. She tenderly touched the needy, making sure that they felt cared for instead of abandoned, even as they took their leave of life. In the documentaries, Mother Teresa speaks for the Loving Mother and says over and over again that a sense of abandonment is the most debilitating experience a person can have, even worse than physical hunger.

4. Love yourself.

As you work to reclaim your Loving Mother archetype, remember you must love yourself first to truly love others. Pay attention to how you care for yourself—body, mind and soul. Make sure you give yourself the same attention you would give to others. Mother your children or children around you, and give that same love to your own child nature.

5. Think positively.

Do not hold back praise for yourself and for others. Remember that what you praise, prospers. Think positively. Hold the highest vision for yourself, others, and every venture you pursue.

6. Appreciate others and be genuine.

Remember that everyone needs to feel appreciated in a genuine way. Catch yourself when you feel like you do not care about someone or something. Show others that you value them for who they are, not for what they do for you. Do not flatter them or compliment them only to get your way. Do not buy their allegiance with money or toys. Be sincere and earnest. Find something nice that you can say about them that is true and then tell them.

7. Pay attention to your internal dialogue.

The Loving Mother always communicates with the words "we, our, us." Notice when you use those nurturing words to explain things to yourself or to others. Learn to communicate using the "who, what, where, when and why." Make sure you have answers to those basic questions when you are trying to understand a situation, so you cover all the bases.

8. Give Loving Mother affirmations.

The following affirmations can help you anchor the presence of the Loving Mother:

I AM my Loving Mother.
I AM teaching, guiding and explaining the
"who,what, when, where and why" of life.
I AM fulfilling all of my needs.
I AM the tenderness, the nearness and the love of
God.
I AM understanding and teaching the law.
I AM nurturing myself and others.

I AM loving myself and others unconditionally.
I AM holding the highest vision for myself and others.
I AM abundance and health in my life.
I AM manifesting the wisdom of the universe.
I AM honoring Father.
I AM nurturing my Boychild and my Girlchild.

Three

Discover What Drives You

Ambition is so powerful a passion in the human breast,
that however high we reach we are never satisfied.
–Longfellow

There is an action principle inside of you that drives everything you do. It can impel you to perform at your best or get you to behave at your worst. It is influenced by an archetype—the Boychild within you.

When your Boychild is loving, he is like a knight in shining armor—glamorous, courageous, fighting for righteous causes. He helps you to excel in life, to accomplish great things and to fulfill your dreams. He joyously understands the wisdom of the Loving Mother and carries out the will of the Loving Father. He likes to get things done right with enthusiasm and verve. He is also a leader, a shepherd who inspires others to follow in his tracks. He has dynamic, charismatic energy, and his charm and sense of humor make him attractive to others.

People who are driven by a strong Boychild archetype want to get to the bottom of every enigma and mystery or at least to the next point. Self-confident, competent and curious, they like to experiment and investigate. The Loved Boychild is all about how—"How do I get this? How does this work? How did this happen?" He believes that once he knows how to do something, he knows everything about it. He can "power-skim," grasp the gist of something very quickly. This skill is similar to speed-reading. He can sort through great quantities of information to find what he is looking for, but he does not always get the full depth of what he is studying, having only skimmed the surface.

The Loved Boychild enjoys games and challenges. He is competitive in mastering skills and plays by the rules, obedient to the Loving Father's directives and disciplines. The Olympic Games are a wonderful display of Loved Boychild sportsmanship, as athletes compete with fair play and team spirit, honoring their sport not only by giving their all but also by wishing their competitors well.

The Loved Boychild is also the sword in the right hand of the Father. He is the warrior; assertive, courageous and fearless in battle. He lives to champion every righteous cause and will carry out the Loving Father's marching orders, come hell or high water. When Boychild is under the aegis and direction of the Loving Father, he will do whatever it takes, face whatever odds and endure to the end.

People who have a strong Boychild tend to be intense, because that is what life expects of them. During World War II, General George Patton was an example of Boychild extraordinaire. Under his leadership, the U.S. army chased the Germans all the way back to Germany. Then, Patton told General Eisenhower that he wanted to take on the Russians and end communism completely and decisively. He needed a green light, a Loving Father directive. Instead,

Eisenhower, who had been aloof to Patton during the whole war, did not cooperate. Had Eisenhower responded otherwise, the history of the twentieth century would have been very different.

The Loved Boychild offers his life for principle—for his family, his country or the world. Most people in uniform have a strong Boychild archetype. When their Loved Boychild is called upon, they will give the ultimate sacrifice, like the New York City firefighters and policemen who lost their lives, evacuating people out of the World Trade Center buildings on September 11, 2001. These are the heroes and heroines who live on in our hearts forever.

When Boychild is driven by selfish agendas and decides to play by his own rules, he becomes a bully. He plays out the unloving side of the Boychild archetype, the rebel who is reckless, angry and aggressive. He disrespects authority. He wants to dominate and will deceive, lie, cheat, backbite and steal to achieve his goals. He sees life as a giant video game and he does not care about who he has to hurt to win. He believes that anyone who steps on his toes or thwarts his agenda deserves an aggressive reaction from him. People who stand in his way, or take what he thinks is his risk paying a big price. When his revenge is delayed, he bides his time until he can get even.

Unloved Boychild is egotistical. He is conceited and likes to use sarcasm. He interrogates to gain control, asking questions that he already knows the answer to, are subjective or have no right to be asked—like "What were you thinking?" He often has a playboy attitude. He is selfish and always places himself first. He wants what he wants when he wants it and demands immediate gratification. He expects maximum return for minimum effort and he can be very ungrateful. He places a utilitarian value on others, always assessing how useful they might be to further his objectives. He also likes to count beans to make sure nobody gets more than he does.

Unloved Boychild is defined by extreme negative competition. He is always measuring who is superior and who is inferior. He has to be better than everyone and everything and to have the last word. He must be the "fastest gun in the West."   Brian had a Boychild client who would even compete with traffic lights. He was sure they were purposely changing red on him, so he took them on and would race through every time.

Our society is driven by Unloved Boychild competition. People call it the law of the jungle, "dog eat dog." Popular television shows like *Survivor* or *The Weakest Link* reflect the collective fascination with Unloved Boychild. The nightly news regularly shows us dominant Boychildren who get away with being bullies in the schoolyard of Earth. "My bomb is bigger than your bomb," "My army can take your army," "My corporation is going to come in and take over your corporation" are common themes.

Most people witnessed with horror the destruction of the World Trade Center buildings in New York City. "How could anyone be capable of this level of hatred and disregard for life?" we wondered. Terror is a tactic of Unloved Boychild, who will stop at nothing to carry out his plans and get his way.

Unloved Boychild is also smart enough to know that he has to create an image for himself or a cause that his followers will buy into. That's how Hitler was able to pull off getting elected and then taking over the

German government. He knew the Germans needed a way to feel good about themselves after their smashing defeat in World War I. He played them by convincing them that he would lead them to glory. Hitler was an example of Unloved Boychild taken to an extreme. People who were close to him said that when he did not get his way, he would bite his hand, throw himself down on the floor, kick and scream, and then somebody would pay.

Boychild's key words are "I, my, mine." The Loved Boychild uses these words to defend his mission. "This is my responsibility," he says. When Unloved Boychild uses these words, he is selfish, combative and threatening. "This is mine," he says, "and you'd better not touch it."

Overcoming selfishness is a difficult issue for anyone with a strong Boychild archetype. Unloved Boychild believes he knows best. He wants his way and thinks that things can only work out if he is in charge and if he can control the circumstances and people in his life. People with a strong Boychild archetype sometimes find it very hard to trust in the universe, to "let go and let God."

The Loved Boychild, on the other hand, submits to the leadership, direction, discipline and boundaries that the Loving Father brings to him instead of doing his own thing to inspire astonishment and admiration from others. He knows that to be a good leader, you must first be a good follower. He embodies the maxim, "I and my Father are one," and submits to the disciplines of life. In so doing, he earns his stripes and becomes authentic.

The 1997 Disney animation *Hercules* is a story about the redemption of our Boychild archetype. After surmounting almost undefeatable odds, Hercules is faced with the most difficult initiation—to put his ego aside for something greater than himself. When he succeeds, he experiences the victory of the Loved Boychild, the hero that dwells in each of us.

Tools to Engage Your Loved Boychild

1. Ask yourself these questions.

The following questions can help you assess the Loved Boychild's presence in your life:

Do you enjoy finding out how things work?
Do you work at something until you are good at it?
Do you explore the unknown?
Are you adventurous?
Do you like playing games or sports?
Do you marvel at other people's competencies?
Do you like to make people laugh?
Do you stand up for your rights and other people's rights?
Are you self-confident most of the time?

If you answered yes to most of these questions, your Loved Boychild is probably quite active. If not, use the tools below to expand his presence in your life and overcome Unloved Boychild behavior.

2. Engage your Loved Boychild.

Allow your Boychild to gain mastery. Engage him within Loving Father parameters so he doesn't go overboard. Set healthy goals for yourself, accomplish those goals and reward yourself in a positive way. Get involved in physical activity. Take a hike, play a team sport or join a health club. Offer to help someone who needs your competency. Get involved in a good cause that means something to you and go the extra mile. Make sure you always finish what you start.

3. Curb your Unloved Boychild.

Notice under what circumstances you express Unloved Boychild. When are you over-competitive and combative? When do you insist on being in charge or want your way at all costs? When do you let yourself get angry? When you recognize that your Unloved Boychild has taken over, choose to be the Loving Father and put the brakes on that behavior. In that moment when your Boychild would get angry, try to step back and become impersonal. Then as the Loving Mother, explain to your Boychild that when he reacts in a negative way, it actually makes him weaker. Remind him that he will be more successful in accomplishing his goals if he does not tread on other people.

4. Monitor your competitiveness.

Analyze how competitive you are. Do you only feel confident if you come out on top or ahead of everyone else?   Do you try to measure up to others or to standards set by the media and the entertainment industry?   Are you motivated by Unloving Father criticism from yourself and others?   If so, it is time to reassess your priorities. Remember that no matter what Boychild does, it will never be good enough for Unloving Father. Stop stressing and go within. Find your inner balance. Center your life around healthy principles and get your marching orders from the Loving Father.

5. Watch out for addictions.

Observe whether you have an addictive tendency. Are you an overachiever? Are you a workaholic? Are you always trying to get more in life, to find the best deal, to get away with whatever you can? Is it hard for you to feel satisfied with what you have? Can you respect other people's boundaries or do you solicit for more than what they would comfortably give—be it money, time, sex or affection? The Loved Boychild respects the boundaries that the Loving Father gives him. He knows when to stop. He knows how to honor other people. Unloved Boychild ignores the Loving Father and recklessly pursues the "mommy" things of life in a frustrated attempt to satisfy his insatiable appetite for connection and pleasure. He always wants more of what he thinks will satisfy him—time, attention, money, material acquisitions, food, alcohol, drugs and sex—but he can never get enough. No one and nothing can fill his void.

6. Pay attention to your internal dialogue.

Watch your tone when you speak from the first person ("I, my, mine.") When you use these words, your Boychild archetype is active, so you can pay attention to what is driving you. Also notice how often you speak about yourself. Is your dialogue loving, empowering and helpful to others or is it self-centered, selfish and destructive? Loved Boychild communicates to shepherd others. Unloved Boychild communicates to manipulate them, so he can get his way.

7. *Give Loved Boychild affirmations.*

The following affirmations can help you anchor the presence of the Loved Boychild:

I AM my Loved Boychild.
I AM courage and fearlessness.
I AM the overcomer.
I AM a conquering hero.
I AM the mastery of life.
I AM the defender of righteousness, justice and peace.
I and my Father are one.
I AM the will of my Father made manifest.

Four

Appreciate Your Muse

Artists have invoked the Muse since time immemorial.
There is great wisdom to this.
There is magic to effacing our human arrogance and
humbly entreating help from a source
we cannot see, hear, touch or smell.
—Steven Pressfield

In the 1960 musical, *Camelot*, Arthur tells Guinevere that when Merlin left Camelot, all the pink left with him. There is an archetype that puts the pink back into our world. It brings finesse, inspiration and magic into our lives, and it makes us cry at every happy ending. This archetype touches us deeply and makes life special. It is extraordinarily complex. It is multidimensional, ineffable and mysterious. Like the Holy Spirit, it cannot be quantified. We call this archetype the Loved Girlchild.

The Loved Girlchild is not easily described, though we wrap many words around her: beauty, sweetness, forgiveness, gentleness, innocence, goodwill, holiness, sensitivity, diplomacy, intuition, compassion and harmlessness.

The Loved Girlchild is our muse, the source of our creative power. She allows us to engage sensitively in life, to hear with our inner voice and to connect with the essence of things. She is our most intimate archetype. She serves as a stepping-stone to Spirit, where, unless you become as a little child, you shall not enter in.* Through her, we contact the transcendental.

When Caroline was a child, she would lay in the snow under a street light to watch the snow fall and would lose herself in the infinity of snow flakes descending from the sky. This was one of the ways she experienced the Loved Girlchild.

The Loved Girlchild fills us with a sense of awe. She is present at every birth, every death and every major change in life. She brings healing and inspiration to our lives. She moves us with beautiful music and art. She opens our hearts. She is the wind beneath our wings. She helps us to shift paradigms and to make the leap between who we are today and who we are meant to become.

The Loved Girlchild thinks in a spherical way. She also finds it hard keeping track of time. People who have a strong Girlchild archetype, like most painters, writers and musicians, can become so absorbed in her magic that they completely lose track of time.

The Latin culture tends to have a strong Girlchild focus. When Therese spent four months in South America, she found that people there generally had different values. They were more gentle, more caring, more appreciative of other people's feelings. They went out of their way to share their blessings and to notice beauty. Relationships were more important than material success, and people spent more time with their families. Most things ran on Latin time and stress was a futile experience.

---

* Mark 10:15

When Therese returned to New York City, she slammed back into Boychild culture. The first thing she noticed when she got off of the plane was a billboard that stated, "You've got 60 seconds, 30 things to do.... We can help." The culture shock she experienced resulted from the juxtaposition of these two archetypal energies.

The Loved Girlchild truly, sincerely cares and wants the best for everybody. She has a strong sacrificial pattern. Her dialogue words are "me, my, mine," but unlike Boychild, when she says, "This is mine," she wants to share.

The Loved Girlchild finishes any situation with finesse, forgiveness and resolution, leaving no strings untied. She crosses every "t" and dots every "i." She makes sure every jot and tittle of the law is fulfilled, or, from an Eastern perspective, that every karma is balanced. She wants everybody to spiritually make it and will seek to save those who seemingly cannot be saved.

In addition to her strong expression of Loving Mother, Mother Teresa had a very developed Loved Girlchild pattern. She worked in the streets of Calcutta with those who were most unwanted, those the newspapers called "the refuse of life." She let them know they were truly and deeply loved. Those who survived were devoted to her for the rest of their lives. Those who passed on were sent with such love it may have been the only time in their earthly lives that they encountered God face to face.

People who have a strong Loved Girlchild archetype have a magic within their nature that tends to attract criticism from others and makes life more difficult. They are often put down and labeled as childish and flaky—incompetent dreamers who care about trifles. However, their strength lies in this seeming weakness. The Loved Girlchild knows that what comes around goes around. She finds peace in her faith that everything works out for the good.

When people who function from their Girlchild archetype do not feel appreciated, they may succumb to her negative counterpart, Unloved Girlchild. Unloved Gilrchild is the wounded victim who whines, complains and is paralyzed by fear. She drowns in self-pity, discouragement and resentment. Manipulative, she seduces others into rescuing her, like a melodramatic soap opera queen. Then, as soon as she is rescued from one drama, she moves into another.

We are all at some level vulnerable to Unloved Girlchild. We fall into her hole every time we react to the negative things other people send our way, every time we find ourselves hurt and unappreciated, every time we say, "After all I've done for them, this is what they do to *me....*" When Unloved Girlchild takes over, we may experience overwhelming pain. We may feel powerless and we are desperate to please.

By responding from Unloved Girlchild, we attract negativity into our lives again and again. That's why many people who operate from their Unloved Girlchild archetype are, in fact, often mentally, emotionally or physically abused. Unloved Girlchild gives us a warped sense of self-righteousness. When she is victimized, she covertly feels superior to those who affront her. She finds comfort—even a spiteful joy—in thinking that those who wound her may be in spiritual jeopardy and are unworthy of her care.

Learning to value our Loved Girlchild requires that we face what we dread most or where we hurt the most, which can be very difficult. People who do not have Girlchild in a dominant archetypal position are often uncomfortable working with her. They seek to avoid the openness and sensitivity that would make them feel vulnerable to attack from others.

We have to be willing to confront Girlchild's pain in order to appreciate what she will bring to us. The day after best-selling author, Margaret Fishback Powers, became engaged, she wrote a poem called *Footprints*—which was one of many poems. Years later, the box in which her poems were stored was lost in a move. She was very disappointed, because her writings were so personal and important to her, but she had to let it go.

Three years later, she came upon a calligraphy of *Footprints* in a Christian bookstore. She was dumbfounded. She spent the next seven years writing to publishing companies about the ownership and the loss of her poem, to no avail.

Margaret became paralyzed by bitterness and by a "what they did to *me*" Unloved Girlchild attitude. She did not know if she could ever write again. Then, one day, she decided to relinquish the issue, to "leave it with the Lord" and to forgive.

Margaret embraced the Loved Girlchild who can forgive when she is affronted. Her change of heart fulfilled an astonishing revelation she had received many years before, that "Forgiveness is the fragrance the blossom leaves on the sole after it has crushed the flower.*"

Margaret reconnected with her muse, and her writer's block ended. She sat down and wrote a book

---

* Margaret Fishback Powers. *Footprints.* New York, N.Y.: Walker and Company, 1998. p. 46

called *Footprints*, which became a bestseller. Though she never won back the rights to her inspired poem, the personal trial she experienced is a witness to its message:

"I'm aware that during the most troublesome times of my life there is only one set of footprints. I just do not understand why, when I needed You most, You leave me." He whispered, "My precious child, I love you and will never leave you, never, ever, during your trials and testings. When you saw only one set of footprints it was then that I carried you."

Like Margaret, when we are willing to forgive and to trust in a greater plan, we can receive the cornucopia of blessings that the Loved Girlchild bestows on those who appreciate her. Our creativity is unleashed, and the Spirit can move through us. People no longer victimize and control us by hurting our feelings. We are authentic. We are free to go on with our lives and the universe rewards us.

Tools to Engage your Loved Girlchild

1. Ask yourself these questions.

The following questions can help you assess the Loved Girlchild's presence in your life:

Are you very sensitive?
Do you care for people and avoid hurting anyone?
Do you try to comfort anyone or anything in pain?
Do you like to finish things with finesse?
Do you get so engaged in something that you forget the time?
Do you believe in things you do not see?
Do you just know or intuit things?
Do you feel a strong sense of self-worth?

"No" answers to any of these questions are cues to the absence of the Loved Girlchild, or the presence of Unloved Girlchild in her stead. If that is so, use the tools below to invite Loved Girlchild into your life and become free of Unloved Girlchild behavior.

2. Do not let Unloved Girlchild drag you down.

Notice what situations trigger your Unloved Girlchild. What makes you feel hurt, rejected, maltreated, devalued or worthless? When these happen, take a step back and summon your Loving Father archetype. Your Loving Father sets the boundaries your Loved Girlchild needs to blossom. He can help her stay focused, objective and rational, so she can break free of Unloved Girlchild's reactive pattern. He reassures her that she is safe, protected and valued for her own sake. Then, invite your Loving Mother to show you why you got hurt and what you can learn from the circumstance. Your Loving Mother can help you explore the meaning of your pain. Your Girlchild will feel nurtured in her presence and be relieved that she no longer has to bear her pain alone. Finally, engage your Loved Boychild to take the necessary action, under the Loving Father's direction and the Loving Mother's guidance, so you no longer attract abuse into your life.

3. Appreciate your muse.

The Loved Girlchild is your muse. She comes forth through creative expression. Unleash your creativity, and she will show you what she likes to do—be it smelling flowers, caring for a baby bird, or writing poetry. Remember that the Loved Girlchild does not like to be constrained. Set her free, do not be judgmental, and watch her talents unfold in your life.

4. Take time to play.

Of all the archetypes, the Loved Girlchild is most childlike. You invite her into your life when you allow yourself to be childlike and carefree. Play with children, skip down a road, stop and smell the flowrs, sing a happy song. Surrender the rigidity of your adult sophistication for a moment, and let your innocent nature come alive.

5. Practice communing with Spirit.

The Loved Girlchild can be your fount of inspiration, your connection with universal consciousness. Attune with her presence as you meditate, pray, talk to God, commune with nature or serve other people. Listen to your inner voice. Honor your intuition. Let the Loved Girlchild's gentle wisdom guide you.

6. Finish everything with finesse.

Few people know how to end with beauty. Try to accomplish your tasks with finesse. Care enough to give the best of yourself. Make an extra effort when you cook a meal, clean your house or get dressed in the morning. Strive for beauty and perfection in your life, even when it seems mundane. Take the time to put loving care into your relationships. Be considerate and treat other people as well as you would like to be treated. Pay special attention to what others say to you, even if it is non-verbal, and try to meet their needs before they even ask. Show people that you want the best for them.

7. Trust in the universe.

Loved Girlchild is the full expression of serendipity. She lives in the moment. She trusts in the universe. She can "let go and let God." She gracefully goes with the flow and takes things as they come. She does not try to preempt her circumstances. She knows the universe will always provide for her, and it does. She surrenders to life with poise and equanimity. The more you practice living this way, the more you will express your Loved Girlchild archetype.

8. Pay attention to your internal dialogue.

Watch your tone when you say "me." Are you coming from the Loved Girlchild or from Unloved Girlchild? Are you complaining or are you humble and matter of fact? Resist the urge to be a victim of life's circumstances and rest assured that when you embrace your Loved Girlchild's selfless and caring nature, all heaven will be behind you.

9. Give Loved Girlchild affirmations.

The following affirmations can help you anchor the presence of the Loved Girlchild in your life:

I AM my Loved Girlchild.
I AM my brother's keeper.
I AM the spirit of hope, faith and charity.
I AM joy and happiness today.
I AM inspired by the universe.
I AM perfect forgiveness.
I AM beautiful and real.
I AM awareness of all aspects of life.
I AM selfless service.
I AM freedom from fear, over-concern and human limitation.
I AM seeking to save the seemingly unsavable.
I AM comforting life.
I AM ending things with beauty.

Part One ~ Key Concepts

Four **principles** can help you to become authentic. They can be summarized as:

1. Drawing your boundaries.
2. Embracing your inner teacher.
3. Discovering what drives you.
4. Appreciating your muse.

These four principles relate to four specific **archetypes** imbedded in everyone's consciousness—the inner Father, the inner Mother, the inner Boychild and the inner Girlchild.

When you function from a loving archetypal behavior, you become your **best self**. You expand your competencies and you enjoy healthy interactions with others. When you yield to negative archetypal behavior, you become your **worst self** and you sabotage your life and your relationships.

Your **loving inner family archetypes** consist of the Loving Father, Loving Mother, Loved Boychild and Loved Girlchild. Your **unloving inner family archetypes** consist of the Unloving Father, Unloving Mother, Unloved Boychild and Unloved Girlchild.

Your **Loving Father** helps you draw boundaries. His job is to protect, direct, discipline and give conditional love. He gives you the impersonality you need to stop taking offense and to overcome challenging situations.

Your **Unloving Father** is your inner critic, the part of you that mercilessly criticizes yourself and other people. He represents the misuse of power.

Until you fully access the Loving Father internally, you can use **alpha grids**—established rules and guidelines—that set a code of conduct for people to follow.

Your **Loving Mother** archetype is your inner teacher. She nurtures, teaches, guides, explains and gives unconditional love. She is very personal and holds the highest thoughts for you. Through the "who, what, when, where and why," she clarifies situations in your life.

Your **Unloving Mother** archetype avoids personal giving. She is either aloof and abandoning, or manifests as smother-mother.

Your **Loved Boychild** archetype drives you. He is your action principle. He is competitive with himself and others and he plays fair. He seeks to know the how of things, and he is adventurous and charming. He is also the good shepherd.

Your **Unloved Boychild** archetype is the aggressive, negative, competitive side of human nature that lies, cheats and steals to win at all costs. He expresses your anger.

Your **Loved Girlchild** archetype is your muse. She is your caring, sensitive, mystical self. She brings finesse, beauty and resolution to your life. She seeks to save the seemingly unsavable.

Your **Unloved Girlchild** archetype is the martyr victim who feels unappreciated. She always says, "After all I've done for you, this is what you do to me." She wants others to appease her, but can never be satisfied.

The goal of **working with your inner family archetypes** is to substitute positive archetypal patterns for negative ones, so that you can become authentic and strengthen your relationships.

Your Best Self

Loved Girlchild

Seeks to save the seemingly unsavable. She cares, beautifies and ends things with finesse. She is joy, freshness, poetry and art.

Loving Father

Protects, directs, disciplines and gives conditional love. He is impersonal and always acts in consort with Loving Mother's unconditional love.

Loving Mother

Nurtures, teaches, guides, explains and gives unconditional love. She is personal.

Loved Boychild

Seeks to find how things work. He is the scientist, explorer, competitor, and wants to master all things.

Your Worst Self

Unloved Girlchild

Seeks to control through the martyr complex. She is the victim who must be appeased.

Unloving Father

Seeks to control through criticism.

Unloving Mother

Seeks to control through abandonment and avoids genuine giving of self. Manifests as aloof or smother-mother behavior.

Unloved Boychild

Seeks to control through division and negative competition. Must win at all costs.

Archetypal Qualities

	Quality	Key Word(s)	Key Function	Key Dialogue Word
Father	IMPERSONAL	DO	DIRECTION	YOU
Mother	PERSONAL	WHO, WHAT, WHERE, WHEN and WHY	PRO-VISION	WE, OUR and US
Boychild	IMPERSONAL and PERSONAL	HOW	ACTION	I, MY and MINE
Girlchild	PERSONAL and IMPERSONAL	CARE	COMFORT, BEAUTY, FINESSE and CONVERSION	ME, MY and MINE

PART TWO

FIVE STEPS TO
SELF-KNOWLEDGE

Five steps can help you to map out your personal archetypal pattern so you can understand exactly how your archetypes play out in your day-to-day life.

The first step is to become aware of your spiritual connection through your superconscious mind. Your spiritual connection is influenced by the archetype you aspire to most.

The second step is to understand your thinking style that plays out through your conscious mind. Your thinking style is influenced by the archetype you reason with.

The third step is to tap your emotions in your subconscious mind. Your emotions are colored by the archetype you feel through.

The fourth step is to discover the sabotaging mechanism in your unconscious mind so you can replace it with your unconscious reservoir of positive potential. This sabotaging mechanism relates to an archetype.

The fifth step is to identify your social mask, the image you were trained to put forth. Your social mask is influenced by the archetype through which you socialize.

Step by step, you will begin to recognize the personal archetypal pattern that you printed and that is ultimately yours to master. You will begin to see how this archetypal pattern shapes the way you think, the way you feel and the way you relate to others. You will begin to notice how this pattern can affect your relationships by influencing the choice of people you are drawn to and the people you naturally tend to dislike.

To recognize your personal archetypal pattern, you need to determine:

1. Which of the four inner family archetypes you aspire to. That is your spiritual archetype. It influences your spiritual connection and abides in your superconscious mind.
2. Which archetype you reason through. That is your thinking archetype. It impacts your reasoning ability and rules your conscious mind.
3. Which archetype you feel through. That is your feeling archetype. It determines your emotional reserve and dwells in your subconscious mind.
4. Which archetype you reject. That is your sabotaging archetype. It creates a sabotaging mechanism deep in your unconscious mind.

Each archetype has one dominant role. If, for instance, you feel through Boychild, you will not think through Boychild. If you aspire to Mother, you will not reject Mother.

Where your Father archetype falls, you know how to draw boundaries and may fall prey to criticism. Where your Mother archetype falls, you are your inner teacher, but you may also have a tendency to be aloof. Where your Boychild archetype falls, you are driven to get things done, but you may also exhibit aggression.

Where your Girlchild archetype falls, you connect with your muse, but you may feel unappreciated.

Once you have figured out your personal archetypal pattern, it is helpful to assess your social mask—the archetype through which you socialize. We call this archetype your socialization archetype. It will be the same as one of your four personal archetypes, and it will also apply to your immediate family.

Five

Accessing Your Spiritual Connection

*The key to growth is the introduction of
higher dimensions of consciousness into our awareness.*
–Lao Tzu

Just beyond your conscious awareness lies your superconscious mind—a storehouse of inspiration and blessing, a wellspring of spiritual healing and solutions to problems that you can tap into. Every time you engage your superconscious mind, you connect with spiritual reality and access higher realms of consciousness. It is like a blueprint over you, waiting to download, offering intuitive guidance, so you can fulfill your mission in life.

The superconscious mind can access all four loving archetypes, but we have learned to emphasize one more than the others. This dominant superconscious archetype is what we call our spiritual archetype. It is the one we aspire to most. No matter what religion or spiritual path we choose to follow—or not to follow—this archetype will depict how we see God.

It is important for us to identify the archetype we aspire to, otherwise, when people come along who represent that archetype for us, we may grant them

God-like status. We may become so enthralled with them that we give all of our power away to them.

If, for example, your superconscious archetype is Boychild, anytime you run into people who have a strong Boychild pattern, they will represent everything you idealize, and you may allow them to define you or take advantage of you. When you know your superconscious archetype and recognize that behavior in others, you will be less drawn in head over heels. You can summon your Loving Father's impersonality and stay objective.

The relationship you had with your parents or primary nurturers during your first three years of life and even in the womb, influenced how you relate to your superconscious archetype. Up until age three, our parents or primary nurturers were God-like figures to us. Their competence was undeniable and their authority unquestioned. We depended on them for everything and could not exist without them. The power they wielded over us, for good or ill, helped mold our superconscious connection. Even though our superconscious archetype is loving, the early disappointments we had with our parents may cause us to see it as unloving. Until we forgive our parents for their shortcomings, we tend to project our childhood grievances onto our superconscious archetype.

To identify your spiritual connection, you need to determine which of the four inner family archetypes dominates your superconscious mind. You can do this by asking the following questions and then choosing which description best fits you.

◆ When you think of God, the Creator, the Universal Force, the Great Spirit, the Source, what comes to mind?
◆ Which inner family archetype do you prefer, do you most admire?
◆ Which archetype would you most like to be?

Superconscious Father

Do you pursue righteousness? Do you aspire to bringing forth principle, justice and fair play into your day-to-day interactions? Do you always want to know where everything stands? Do you sometimes feel that laws and rules are arbitrary and go against you, or that God is criticizing you and that the universe is very harsh and unfair? If so, Father may be your superconscious archetype.

Superconscious Loving Father's objective is to put forth a blueprint that will protect, direct and discipline people. If your dominant spiritual archetype is the Loving Father, you pursue righteousness. You aspire to bringing forth principle, justice and fair play in your day-to-day interactions with others. You tend to be entrepreneurial and autonomous. You always want to know where everything stands. You may also have a concentrated masculine energy about you, which protects you from getting pushed around.

When you project Unloving Father criticism and tyranny onto your superconscious archetype, this can be devastating, because you feel like you have nowhere to hide. His omnipresence gives you the sense that the universe is a very harsh and unfair place—where might is right and where universal law favors the powerful over the vulnerable and innocent.

Superconscious Mother

Are you looking for unconditional love from God and from others? Do you strive to guide and nurture others by teaching the "who, what, where, when and why" of things? Do you sometimes find it easier to love humanity than to love people one-on-one? Does the universe seem to withhold its nurturance and abundance from you when you are having a rough time? If so, you could have a superconscious Mother archetype.

If the Loving Mother is your dominant spiritual archetype, you aspire to guide, nurture and love others unconditionally. You aspire to explain the "who, what, where, when and why" of things and can develop a lot of competence in this area.

You want God to teach and nurture you and you expect unconditional love. You tend to believe that happiness is having all of your wants fulfilled, and you may be overly materialistic. When life's challenges come to your doorstep, you tend to balk. You would rather ignore the karmic law that says you must reap what you have sown. You see life as "feast or famine." When the universe seems to withhold its nurturance and abundance from you, you project Unloving Mother aloofness onto your superconscious Mother archetype. Then, everything becomes cold and dry to you, and you feel abandoned by God for not getting what you want.

Superconscious Boychild

Do you aspire to be a hero and to champion causes even when you lack the wherewithal to make things happen? Do you believe you have a destiny to carry out even if you are insecure about making it happen?

Can you become fanatical about your ideals? Do you relate to God as a savior who is there for you in a personal way? If so, you may have a superconscious Boychild archetype.

If the Loved Boychild is your dominant spiritual archetype, you aspire to be a hero who rescues others. You want to gain control over your environment and show forth mastery. You would rather not pursue mundane preoccupations, because you believe you have a divine destiny to carry out. You tend to see God as a conquering champion like Jesus, David or Krishna. You also want a personal savior who is right there for you, and you will readily accept that savior into your life.

When you allow Unloved Boychild behavior to color your superconscious archetype, your zeal becomes destructive and you may become fanatical in the name of God. Then, it is hard for you to temper your ambitions, because you are convinced that you are in the right.

Superconscious Girlchild

Do you aspire to beauty and finesse? Do you want God to manifest as Spirit moving through life? Do you sometimes like to suffer for the sake of suffering? Do other people sometimes take advantage of you or swindle you in business? If you answer yes, you may have a superconscious Girlchild archetype.

If the Loved Girlchild is your dominant spiritual archetype, you aspire to beauty, finesse and sensitivity. You want to know the hidden side of life, and you expect that your efforts will reveal great mysteries to you. You may also pursue the overwhelming, ecstatic, transforming love that happens when you come into direct contact with Spirit and then strive to convert others.

You can be vulnerable to charlatans if you do not learn to distinguish between charismatic emotionalism and the actual presence of the divine spirit in your life. Differentiating between the two is all the more difficult if you associate Unloved Girlchild with your superconscious archetype, because your understanding of spiritual sacrifice becomes warped. You believe that by punishing yourself, you can become a spiritual martyr. You end up suffering only for the sake of suffering and you do not accomplish anything constructive.

✦

Knowing which of the inner family archetypes is your spiritual archetype helps you better understand what you aspire to. It helps you to recognize those qualities you are especially drawn to in other people. It also helps you to become more aware of your spiritual connection. The more you can tune into the archetype that rules your superconscious mind, the more you can invoke the power of Spirit to work positive change in your life and call down the superconscious blueprint that offers a loving solution for every circumstance.

We connect with our superconscious archetype through the heart. The more you will practice listening to the still, small voice of your conscience that speaks through your heart, the more you will access the wisdom of your superconscious mind and your spiritual archetype. Listening to that prompting will help you become authentic and relate to people in the best possible way.

Six

Understanding Your Thinking Style

We are what we think.
All that we are arises with our thoughts.
With our thoughts, we make the world.
—Gautama Buddha

Your thinking style is influenced by the archetype that dominates your conscious mind. This archetype is your thinking archetype. Through it, your mental faculties naturally function. From about the time you are fifteen years old, your thinking archetype becomes the primary archetype you use. It can describe how you use your free will to act in life and how you behave in an intellectual and professional environment.

We don't run into people who have a conscious Father archetype. That is because the Father archetype is not automatically printed at the conscious level. The attributes of Loving Father have, for the most part, not been passed on from generation to generation. The Loving Father's impersonality and stern code of conduct make us uncomfortable, and his boundaries and discipline can be challenging to enforce.

There is a collective fear of Father lodged in what Carl Jung called the collective unconscious[*]. We associate Father energy with criticism, and we believe that if we make a mistake, he will send us to hell. That is why Father energy can seem intimidating, even when it is loving. If, for instance, we get pulled over by a police officer for not wearing our seat belt, our heart may beat faster, because we are confronted with archetypal Father—an encounter with the law. This can make us so uncomfortable that we want to avoid it at all costs.

It is important for us to reacquaint ourselves with Loving Father energy. Little by little, as you practice the exercises in Chapter One, you can learn to consciously anchor his archetypal qualities, and he will reinforce your thinking archetype with protection, direction, discipline and impersonality.

To identify your thinking style, you need to determine which of the remaining three inner family archetypes (Mother, Boychild or Girlchild) dominates your conscious mind. You can do this by asking yourself the following questions and then choosing the archetype that best suits you.

◆ Which of the archetypes do you most identify with?
◆ Which archetype do you most function from in your day-to-day life?
◆ Which archetype seems most familiar to you?

---

[*]
Jung, C.G.. *The archetypes and the collective unconscious* (R.F.C. Hull, Trans.). Princeton University Press. 1969

Conscious Boychild

Are you competitive? Do you have a drive to get things done? Do you have a good sense of humor and a lot of zeal? Can you become aggressive or overcompetitive? If so, you may have a conscious Boychild archetype.

If Boychild is your dominant thinking archetype, you are likely to be a "go-getter," a mover and a shaker in life. Nothing stops you. You have a lot of energy. You are expedient and competent. You probably drive fast. You always want to know how things work and how they fit into the system. You want quick results, and you may leave things unfinished. You like to "power-skim" situations, to grasp the gist of something very quickly.

Conscious Boychild also gives you a lot of charisma and a good sense of humor. You have a strong personality and you can be very persuasive and enthusiastic. You want to be in charge and may become mentally arrogant or even aggressive when the unloved side of Boychild takes over. You like to be the center of the universe, and you want what you want when you want it, which sometimes makes it harder for you to get along with others.

Conscious Mother

Are you methodical in how you do things? Do you like to make sure all of your bases are covered? Do you respond to situations in a wise, contained, adult manner? Do you tend to mother other people? When you are not happy, do you either become aloof or overindulge others? If so, Mother could be your conscious archetype.

If your dominant thinking archetype is Mother, you naturally like to teach and to nurture life. You typically look for the "who, what, where, when and why" to explain any situation. You have been trained to relate in an adult fashion—calm, restrained, mature and polite. You like to be in control of your emotions and you behave in a way that is considerate of others. You expect everyone else to do the same for you, and you may become aloof to those who do not comply with the standards you set. You may also find it difficult to be under the authority of people who have a conscious Boychild or Girlchild archetype.

Other people tend to rely on your innate adultness. Your Mother energy makes you trustworthy in their eyes. You seem highly competent, and people gravitate to your wisdom.

Conscious Girlchild

Do you like to engage your creative side all of the time? Are you naturally gentle and forgiving? Do you want to care for everyone? Is it hard for you to stay focused or on time? Are you often misunderstood or brutalized by others? Do you respond by complaining or by becoming resentful? If so, you may have a conscious Girlchild archetype.

When Girlchild is your dominant thinking archetype, you want to make things beautiful and you incorporate care into everything you do. You are always aware of the emotional impact you have on others. You seek to save people that everyone else has given up on. You do not think in a linear way, and you are very much in touch with Spirit.

Girlchild is like a chameleon, changing colors to reflect what other people want from her. Because she is the most malleable and unchallenging archetype, she does not always know what to do unless she is told what to do. This makes it easy for people who have a conscious Girlchild to get pushed around.

When Unloved Girlchild takes over, you may display a strong inferiority complex. You may continually justify your way of seeing things, and you are often met with misunderstanding. You often feel victimized until you learn to stop letting other people get to you. Only then can your Loved Girlchild thrive and make magic happen in your life.

✦

Because you use your thinking archetype to reason through, it becomes the inner family archetype that is most familiar to you. Once you identify it, you will also be able to tell which archetypes are less familiar to you. Then, you can practice expressing the archetypal qualities that are less developed in you until you can consciously access the strengths of your four loving archetypes anytime.

There are times when you will want to embody the Loved Boychild, who is exuberant, joyful and funny. In other instances, you are needed to nurture and teach with the Loving Mother. Situations may call for you to be sweet and caring through the Loved Girlchild. Others require the Loving Father to draw boundaries and respond in an impersonal way. The following vivid examples demonstrate various situations that call for you to reason through different archetypes.

A little girl rides down the driveway on her bicycle onto the street and is hit by a car. She is rushed to the hospital where there are only three surgeons capable of helping her. One is on sabbatical, another is on the golf course and the third one is on his way home when he gets the emergency call to return to the hospital. He quickly scrubs up and snaps on his gloves. As he walks into the operating room, he sees his daughter lying on the table.

If he relies on his Mother archetype, he will not be decisive enough to act quickly. If he relies on his Boychild archetype, he will be too personally invested in the outcome, his adrenaline will be rushing, and he will likely make a mistake. If he relies on his Girlchild archetype, he will become overemotional and will not be able to function effectively. His only recourse is his Loving Father archetype.

Surgeons are not permitted to operate on their next of kin, but this doctor realizes that if he does not step up to the plate, his daughter may not live by the time another surgeon arrives on the scene. The Loving Father knows that in this situation, the spirit of the law is more important than the letter of the law. Like this doctor, you can also meet challenging situations with the most appropriate archetype.

Now imagine you come across a little girl in a department store who got separated from her mother. She is sitting on the floor, crying. If you function from Girlchild, you might identify so strongly with her that you feel helpless and overwhelmed. But if you choose to tap into your Loving Mother archetype, you will have the wherewithal to help her find her mother.

Now consider you are walking through a park and two boys are playing Frisbee. The Frisbee goes over one boy's head and flies straight for your head. If Unloved Girlchild takes over, chances are that no matter which way you run, the Frisbee will hit you. But if you can access your Loved Boychild, you'll simply snap it up and throw it back.

When you come around the corner and see a couple of teenagers vandalizing your car, the Loving Father is your best option. His no-nonsense energy will stop the boys in their tracks. If, however, it is a holiday and you need to find the perfect greeting card, you should access your Loved Girlchild archetype. Her sense of care and finesse will make sure you pick the right card every time. Again, the goal is to stop being limited by your archetypal pattern. Instead, you can engage your free will and consciously reason from all four loving archetypes even if, initially, it takes more work. The effort you invest will empower you to respond to situations in an optimal way every time.

Jeffrey found himself in a challenging situation when a client called him up and said, "I have to have a massage appointment with you today." Jeffrey had been working on setting boundaries and replied, "Sorry, I do not have any time. I'm busy and you can call back, and we will set another appointment."
"I cannot believe you're telling me this," the woman answered. "I've known you for years." "Thank you very much," was his only reply.

Later, Jeffrey saw the woman, and she was extremely hostile to him. He told her, "<u>We</u> can work this out. <u>I</u> am going through a cycle where I'm having to learn to set my boundaries, and <u>you</u> can help <u>me</u> do that if <u>you</u> want!" This took her by surprise. "Well, of course I want to help you," she said.

In his conversation with this person, Jeffrey used all of his loving archetypes. He started out with the presence of the Loving Mother through her dialogue word, we, followed by the Loved Boychild, I; then he went to the Loving Father, you, and the Loved Girlchild, me, and finished up with the Loving Father, you. Because he lovingly stated his purpose through each archetype, her aggression melted away.

Knowing which inner family archetype you think through helps you understand why you consciously behave the way you do most of the time. It shows you the groove you naturally run to with its positive and negative consequences. Once you determine to consciously practice all four loving archetypes, no matter what thinking archetype dominated you earlier, you can become more resourceful in how you deal with situations.

Depending on the need of the hour, you can choose to exercise the Loving Father's impersonality. You can exhibit the Loving Mother's wisdom and her nurturing and unifying presence. You can drum up the Loved Boychild's courage or his charm, sense of humor and ability to get others to rally around him. You can also impart the Loved Girlchild's deep sense of caring. You have a wider palette to choose from, and you become more competent.

Learning to consciously express all four loving archetypes can take time, but with every attempt, you anchor a little more of their presence and become more authentic. You do not have to automatically react to recurring circumstances the ways you always have. You can shun unloving archetypal coping mechanisms and strategically choose the best loving archetype for every event and person that crosses your path.

Seven

Tapping Your Emotions

The happiness of a man in this life
does not consist in the absence
but in the mastery of his passions.
–Alfred Lord Tennyson

Emotions run strong, and they are colored by an archetype. This archetype is your feeling archetype. It influences how you relate to people in an intimate way. It determines your comfort zone and reveals how you behaved as a child. Your feeling archetype dwells in your subconscious and often bypasses your free will. It reacts automatically to situations without conscious input and does not respond to reason. You fall back on it when you feel pressured.

Children mainly function from their feeling archetype until they hit puberty. Then, between the ages of eight and fifteen, they function more and more through their conscious archetype, (though flashes of this archetype may appear earlier). The change they experience as they switch between their emotional urge and their reasoning ability is one of the reasons why adolescence can be such a challenging rite of passage. When we look at childhood pictures, we can see that the quality or tone we embodied in our early childhood years (subconscious archetype) changed as we headed into our teenage years (conscious archetype). By the time we become adult, we look different and our essence has changed, archetypically speaking.

To identify your emotional reserve, you need to determine which of the four inner family archetypes dominates your subconscious mind. You can do this by asking the following questions and then choosing which description best fits you.

◆ Which archetype are you most like when you are alone, in private or when you are intimate with someone?
◆ Which archetype are you most like when you are scared, stressed or burdened?
◆ Which archetype do you most feel like when you connect with your emotional self?
◆ Which archetypal characteristics sometimes make you feel immature?

Subconscious Father

Do you have a need for strong principles, discipline and order? Do you desire to rule in any situation but do not always have the wherewithal to carry it out? Are you hypercritical with yourself and thrive on severe discipline? As a child, were you severely criticized whenever you made a mistake, and were you treated like you should have already grown up? If so, you may have a subconscious Father archetype.

If Father is your dominant feeling archetype, you may have a need for strong principles, discipline and order. You want to rule in any situation, but you do not always have the wherewithal to carry it out. You may also feel very besieged. You may have had an unusually difficult childhood where you were severely criticized for every mistake. When you start to tap into your subconscious thoughts and feelings, it is like opening up Pandora's box.

As a result, you may be very harsh with yourself and even hypercritical, self-absorbed and depressed. It may seem like nothing you do is ever good enough for your subconscious Unloving Father. You often embrace what others would see as excessive self-discipline, especially later in life, which may serve you well but tends to put off other people.

Having Father in the subconscious is also a blessing. Because the subconscious is close to the conscious mind, you can consciously access the qualities of your Loving Father archetype more easily than those who do not have a subconscious Father placement. You are an expert at setting and enforcing boundaries, and you can inspire and teach others to do likewise.

Subconscious Boychild

Do you feel competitive, even if you do not act on your competitive drive? Are you comfortable when you feel in control of a situation? As a child, were you tough, very active and sometimes combative? This could mean you have a subconscious Boychild archetype.

If Boychild is your dominant feeling archetype, it may seem that when you were a child, you were in competition with one or both of your parents and that you lost. This felt like a defeat. Later in life, you do whatever you can to avoid being ruled by others.

Boychild in the subconscious gives you an emotional drive to control and accomplish. You innately search out things that are interesting and exciting, and you have a certain joie de vivre. When you automatically engage your subconscious Boychild archetype, you seek to covertly dominate situations, orchestrating his agenda from the back corner of the room. You also have a very strong gut instinct that can help you excel in your area of competency.

Subconscious Mother

Do you feel nurturing, mature and adult deep down inside? Do you become aloof when your feelings are hurt? As a child, did you take on a lot of responsibility? Did people treat you as a little grown-up and expect you to meet some of their needs? If so, you may have a subconscious Mother archetype.

If Mother is your dominant feeling archetype, you have an innate ability to look after others, but you may also have strong childhood abandonment issues. As children, most people who have a subconscious Mother archetype were expected to nurture their parents and family in some way, and did not feel they received the nurturing they needed. If this applies to you, you may have suffered from the pressure of having to take on grown-up responsibilities at an early age, and you coped by becoming aloof to the demands others placed upon you.

Later in life, you can either be emotionally nurturing when you operate from the Loving Mother or refuse to take care of yourself when Unloving Mother takes over. Your gift to life is your innate adult composure, reserve and maturity, which can always be accessed and which help you respond well in times of crisis.

Subconscious Girlchild

Are you extremely sensitive emotionally? Do you cry a lot, even at the movies? Do you care deeply about things? As a child, did you like to daydream? Did you often get picked on and teased? Were you gentle at heart? If so, your subconscious archetype may be Girlchild.

If Girlchild is your dominant feeling archetype, you were probably sweet, well behaved and vulnerable as a child. You may have loved to sing, write poetry and create art. Others expected you to inspire them, comfort them and make them feel good or simply to comply with their expectations.

People with subconscious Girlchild were usually the victim of some aggression and were trained not to challenge authority. When they become stressed, they feel inadequate and overwhelmed. They can exhibit a martyr complex, especially when subconscious Girlchild senses that she is being criticized, rejected or bullied.

Subconscious Girlchild uses her intuition to assess things—what another person might be thinking or whether or not a situation is safe. This intuition can get you into trouble. If you do not develop a certain amount of discretion, people will continuously challenge you to back your assessments with reason, and you may not be able to defend how you know what your Girlchild is telling you.

✦

Understanding your feeling archetype helps you to determine your emotional reserve. It shows you how you behave when you are spontaneous, when you are tired or when you are caught off guard. It indicates how you run on "automatic pilot."

When you function through your feeling archetype, you are reacting from your emotions. Emotions are very powerful. It is important to listen to what they are saying, so they do not become repressed. It is also important to keep in mind that even though they clamor for attention, they are not infallible, and they can steer you off course. To be constructive, they must be filtered through your conscious, thinking archetype. Better yet, you can solicit assistance from your spiritual archetype. When you center on your heart for a superconscious solution instead of relying on your subconscious "gut," you can receive more objective and beneficial feedback.

People often find themselves divided between their thinking and feeling archetypes and end up doing whatever comes easiest. Emotions have such a strong gravitational pull that we feel like we cannot help ourselves. If, for example, we consciously decide to diet, our feeling archetype may protest, "I scream, you scream, we all scream for ice cream," and it is used to getting its way.

Assessing your emotional reserve through your feeling archetype is empowering. When you are confronted with a challenge, you do not have to be childish and let an unloving archetypal program run the show. Instead, you can be authentic. You can engage your free will and choose the loving archetype that will most appropriately deal with each situation in an adult and competent way.

Eight

Overcoming Your Sabotaging Mechanism

Everything that irritates us about others
can lead us to an understanding of ourselves.
–Carl Jung

The unconscious mind is where your sabotaging mechanism resides. It houses your rejected self, the part of yourself that you do not want to own, choose to ignore and project onto people you dislike. The archetype that dominates your unconscious mind is your sabotaging archetype. It blocks your efforts to become authentic. It can undermine your life by pushing you to act in negative ways in spite of yourself, and by preventing you from nurturing healthy relationships with people you initially dislike.

In extreme situations, people who give themselves over to their sabotaging mechanism may completely lose control, as in a war, when the so-called "madness" takes over. This was seen in the war with Iraq when an American soldier followed an impulse to set off a grenade in three tents of fellow sleeping soldiers[*].

Our sabotaging archetype reflects our greatest vulnerabilities, the personal limitations that trip us up,

---

[*] Matthew Cox. *Army identifies soldier killed by comrade's grenade attack.* www.ArmyTimes.com, March 23, 2003

and that we prefer to ignore. We generally do not want to take accountability for the message it sends to others or for the unconscious image it projects about us. When other people confront us with our unconscious behavior, we disown it and reject their feedback. The funny thing is that the more we reject our sabotaging archetype, the more other people wear it for us, right in our face. Their behavior will mimic the sabotaging behavior that we have walled off from our conscious awareness.

Whenever we bump into people who represent our rejected self, they irritate us in a very precise way and bring out the worst in us, *because we are hating ourselves through them*. Jeffrey, who has a conscious Boychild and an unconscious Girlchild archetype, had to work with Pamela, who had the reverse pattern—a conscious Girlchild and an unconscious Boychild archetype. They could never work together harmoniously, because they continually confirmed the negative in each other. Jeffrey thought that if Pamela would just stop whining, everything would be fine. Meanwhile, Pamela kept telling Jeffrey that if he would stop being a dominant bully, there would not be a problem.

Until we purge ourselves of the non-forgiveness we have for ourselves that is reflected in our unconscious unloving archetype, we cannot resolve our differences with others or experience a sense of peace. When we start owning our rejected self, we no longer unconsciously empower other people to get on our nerves, and we can deal justly and impersonally with those who represent our sabotaging archetype.

Brian's client David liked to lie down on a couch to talk, rather than sit at a table. One day, in the middle of a session, while David was sharing some very sensitive information, there were suddenly two knocks on the door. A rowdy young man, who lived three apartments down from Brian's office, burst in. There was only some light shelving separating Brian from the couch where David was talking.

"Yes?" Brian said, caught off guard. He had met this intruder before, when one night he had to go knock on his door and ask him to turn down his wild party music.

"What are you doing in here?" the man said. "You've got people coming and going from here all the time. They come in looking mad or sad, and they come out and they're all googey."

"We're having a meeting, and you are going to have to leave," Brian said firmly, trying to shield his hypersensitive client.

"Oh yeah, who's going to make me?" the man threatened, starting to work his way around the shelving. Brian knew it was time to bring up the best Loving Father archetype he could muster. He escorted his uninvited guest out of the office and closed the door. He could feel his unconscious Boychild pressing in for a fight, and it was all he could do to stay impersonal.

Outside, the young man confided, "I got a girlfriend drunk and she tried to kill herself, and I told her to do it. She was whining and sniveling about this and that, and I said, 'Well, why don't you just go and blow your brains out.' She didn't go and blow her brains out, but she took a whole bunch of pills and they just caught her in time."

Then, Brian realized that this man represented his own unconscious Boychild energy. As this man's Unloved Boychild impatiently trespassed every boundary, it brought Brian's rejected self right into Brian's office. Brian was able to summon his Loving Father and become impersonal, rather than simply react to the unconscious Boychild energy that was set off in him by the incident. This allowed him to see through this man's aggressive behavior and perceive that he really wanted some help but did not know how to ask for it.

To identify your sabotaging mechanism, you need to determine which of the four inner family archetypes dominates your unconscious mind. You can do this by asking the following questions and then choosing the description that best fits you.

◆ Which archetype do you have the most difficulty identifying with?
◆ Which archetypal characteristics do you least admire?
◆ Which archetypal qualities do you find most irritating in others?
◆ Which archetype best describes people who get on your nerves?

Unconscious Father

Are you someone who cannot stand being criticized and controlled and yet you tend to do this to others? Do you often compare yourself to others to assess whether life is fair? Do you feel like you often get the raw end of the deal? Do you find it hard to belong or to integrate into a system? Do you tend to draw criticism from authority figures? If so, you may have the Father archetype in the unconscious.

If Father is your dominant sabotaging archetype, you know how to garner a lot of power and adulation from others, so you can get what you want. You also tend to criticize others and require that they submit to your will. Ironically, you have an extreme aversion to being criticized and controlled, but you magnetize these conditions into your life.

You may also be angry with God. You may find the rules of life unfair. You are always checking to see if somebody else is getting something for nothing, or at least more than you, so you can outwit the perceived favoritism of a seeming blind, arbitrary God. Those who have what you think should be yours receive the critical projection of your unconscious Father.

You often feel like you do not belong and have difficulty integrating with others. You tend to believe that rules do not fit or apply to you and are only there to corral and crush you. As a result, you tend to draw criticism from authority figures that expect you to go along with what they say.

Unconscious Boychild

Do you secretly crave admiration and astonishment from others? Do you shirk away from competition but end up in competitive situations anyway? Are you someone who does not want to be combative and yet continually magnetizes aggressive, arrogant behavior from others? If so, you may have an unconscious Boychild archetype.

If Boychild is your dominant sabotaging archetype, you crave to inspire astonishment and admiration but refuse to admit it. You dislike competition and combativeness but continuously magnetize aggressive, arrogant behavior from others.

Unloved Boychild in the unconscious can also be dangerous. When he comes out, he may become extremely aggressive and out of control. People who are usually very calm and collected and then, for no apparent reason, fall into a fit of rage may have an unconscious Boychild archetype. These people need to learn to harness their unconscious Boychild warrior energy when they encounter uncalled-for aggression from others. They must learn to take a deep breath, bide their time and resist the urge to fall into Unloved Boychild's unconscious combativeness.

Unconscious Mother

Do other people abandon you or seem to abandon you? Do you dislike people who are aloof and yet continually run into them? Do you give up on yourself or on others when your nurturing is most needed? If so, you may have an unconscious Mother archetype.

If your dominant sabotaging archetype is Mother, you expect other people to nurture you, but you behave in a way that precludes it. Your self-sabotaging mechanism demands that other people, one way or another, let you down or abandon you. You strongly dislike people who are aloof and yet continuously draw them into your life. You tend to give up on others when they are in a crunch and most need your assistance. Similarly, you tend to let yourself down by ignoring your need for the Loving Mother. It is important for you to take the time to nurture yourself. When you do this, you will not be as dependent on getting that nurturance from others, and you will not magnetize so much abandonment to yourself.

Unconscious Girlchild

Are you extremely competent but, when something goes awry, you tend to blame somebody else? Are you easily irritated by people who "whine," especially when they say you wronged them? Do you lack respect for people who are intuitive, spontaneous and go the extra mile for others? Are you annoyed when they take up seemingly lost causes? Do you judge them to be too flighty? If so, you may have an unconscious Girlchild archetype.

If Girlchild is your dominant sabotaging archetype, you like to create scapegoats. You are extremely competent and look for someone who can wear your rejected Girlchild for you. When that person comes along, you wait for that person to make a few mistakes and then you "pin the tail on the donkey."

You cannot stand "sniveling whiners," whose feelings get hurt at the drop of a hat, but you attract them into your life. Then, they team up against you to take you down. Every apology you give is further proof to them that you victimized them. The only way out is to become the Loving Father, to stay impersonal, to look at what they are saying and to genuinely try to be fair.

In situations where Unloved Girlchild in the unconscious completely takes over, a person could take their life, as an ultimate act of sabotage and as a guilt trip on others and on society as a whole.

✦

Finding out which inner family archetype sabotages you is extremely helpful. It can help you understand why you experience great difficulty with certain people or situations, and it offers a solution. Every single time someone comes into your life representing your sabotaging archetype, you can be grateful because they are showing you a side of yourself that you need to start owning.

Once you understand that what you cannot stand in others represents what is buried deep within you, you become more compassionate with yourself and with others. As you learn to take responsibility for your suppressed, unconscious behavior, you start appreciating those who outwardly express your sabotaging archetype and mirror your rejected self back to you. Doing this opens the door to new, authentic, meaningful relationships that would never have been possible otherwise.

Nine

Identifying Your Social Mask

*A man's manners are a mirror
in which he shows his portrait.
–Johann Wolfgang von Goethe*

When you were a little child, you learned to socialize by watching your parents or nurturers. You took on a specific pattern from them through which you relate to others. This socialization pattern is part of your "family myth," a set of cherished beliefs sustained by your family. It is a filter through which you relate to others and through which others perceive you. It creates a mask that can weaken your ability to be authentic.

When people first get acquainted, they tend to relate family myth to family myth. They may not be authentic, because the message they are sending out about themselves may not be who they really are. It is only who they were trained to appear like. They may experience love at first sight, until the mask drops. Then, they find themselves saying, "Well, you're not who you pretended to be when we first met," and they feel disappointed. Or they may immediately dislike someone they meet for the first time and later start liking that person.

Our social mask has a dominant inner family archetype. This archetype is our socialization archetype. It flavors how we express ourselves to the world. Because it is the first impression we give, most people think our socialization archetype is our conscious archetype.

Sometimes they are the same. If our conscious archetype is Boychild and we have a Boychild social mask, there is no discrepancy—we come across with a strong Boychild. When our socialization archetype is different from our conscious archetype, we may catch people off guard, because we are not who we initially appeared to be. People whose socialization archetype is the same as their sabotaging archetype encounter the greatest challenge. They have been trained to socially behave like the archetype which gives them the most grief. In every social situation they walk into, they invite people to relate to them through their rejected self. They end up always surrounded by behavior they dislike, because they have been trained to continuously solicit it in others.

Our socialization archetypes are passed on from generation to generation. When two people with the same socialization archetype have children, the archetype that dominates their family myth will transfer to the next generation. If they have different socialization archetypes, the stronger myth is passed on, and the weaker myth becomes dormant.

Brian's mother came from a family with a Mother family myth; his father came from a family with a Boychild family myth. His father's Boychild myth dominated and was passed on to him. When Brian and Therese came together, both of them had a Boychild family myth. This myth was automatically passed on to their children. Now, their children socialize through a Boychild mask.

The more you pay attention to your social mask, the more you can learn to make the most of your family myth and put your best foot forward in every situation. To identify your social mask, you need to determine which of the four inner family archetypes dominates your family myth. You can do this by asking the following questions and then choosing which description best fits you.

◆ Which archetype did your family most admire?
◆ What archetype behaviors did your father and mother reward the most?
◆ In your family stories, which archetype was represented as the "good" one?
◆ Which archetype was favored in the standard instructions you received for presenting yourself in public?

Boychild Family Myth (Most Common)

Are you gregarious, magnetic, outgoing, impetuous, interruptive and exciting in social situations? Do you cruise and schmooze? Are you the life of the party? If so, you may have a Boychild social mask and family myth.

In Western societies, Boychild family myths are the most common. People with a Boychild socialization archetype appear to be Boychild and activate Boychild energy in others. They have a certain flashiness about them. They are very gregarious and they get involved in all kinds of activities. They find great joy in action, competition and social climbing—be it in sports, political races or "Who's Who."

They are very outgoing and like to speak up. They immediately notice how well people are relating to each other and whether they fit in. They tend to survive in any environment. They have a strong entrepreneurial spirit and are often very successful. When their competitive edge turns negative, they engage in a lot of family, sibling and social rivalry and spend much time fighting against others.

People who have a Boychild thinking archetype underneath their Boychild family myth appear to be supreme socializers but often fall short of the mark. In a conversation, they tend to be impatiently thinking about what they are going to say next rather than listening to what the speaker is saying. Communication can break down, because they only grasp the gist of what is being said and may therefore inaccurately interpret what has been said. When many people with this double Boychild combination end up in a room together, there can be so many misinterpretations that everybody starts fighting!

People who have a feminine (Mother or Girlchild) thinking archetype under their Boychild family myth have an advantage in the art of listening and can really talk with people. They enjoy sharing with others so much that it is sometimes hard for them to know when it is time to stop.

Mother Family Myth (Common)

Are you an observer in social situations? Do you like to summarize what other people have said and express it? Do you like to keep a group cohesive and become its adviser? Are you able to be adult, to listen and withhold the need for instant gratification? Do you only enjoy competition if it is in good taste? If so, you may have a Mother social mask and family myth.

Families with a Mother myth are less common than Boychild family myths, but they are still widespread. People who socialize through a Mother archetype are instructive, sophisticated, nurturing and caretaking. They prefer working behind the scenes. They like to retain the wisdom of a group. They also like to gather wisdom and share it with others. They tend to analyze everything through a logical, orthodox framework.

Mother myth families tend to be pillars in their communities and often sponsor the arts, foundations and other philanthropic projects. They have a certain sophistication, etiquette, bearing and care. They relate with adult composure and expect others to do likewise. They are competent, polite, considerate and a little reserved. They tend to follow the norm and respond to cues from others. They are comfortable in groups as long as there is a code of conduct. Under pressure, they may become aloof.

When their family myth is unloving, aloofness takes over. They can be standoffish, cold and rigid. Visiting their home is like walking into a mausoleum. There is no personal touch, no personal giving, no earnestness. They only care about superficiality—what the neighbors think, for example.

Girlchild Family Myth (Rare)

Are you eccentric in social situations? Are you a wallflower, a pariah, a scapegoat or a social castaway? Do you always understand the sorrows and sufferings of others? Are you empathetic, even sympathetic to their plight? If so, you may have a Girlchild social mask and family myth.

People who have a Girlchild socialization archetype are more rare to come by. They genuinely care for others and especially for the downtrodden or anyone worse off than they are. They may take in stray dogs and cats, or even hitchhikers and homeless people.

Families with the Girlchild myth cannot be easily pinned down. They have been trained to project themselves through the ineffableness of Girlchild in a way that may have nothing to do with who they are. They learn to change masks for each person they talk to, because Girlchild adapts to every new situation like a chameleon. They may appear demure and easygoing when they are really determined and strong, or even a bit crazy, when they are in fact quite competent. They have to make an extra effort for people to see through their facade and appreciate them for who they really are.

To outsiders, families with the Girlchild myth relate through chaos. Everything is non-linear, hard to define, intuitive and unpredictable. Nothing is what it seems, and everyone must find creative solutions to survive. Pamela, one of Caroline's clients, experienced this type of chaos as a child before she was given up for adoption. Even though her adoptive family was stable, the only way she knew to get attention, control and a sense of security was by destabilizing her environment through the Girlchild socialization archetype she modeled after in her early years.

Like Blanche DuBois in the 1951 motion picture, *A Streetcar Named Desire*, people with a Girlchild myth always "count on the kindness of strangers" but are often attacked. In social situations, they tend to either draw out the very best in people or their criticism and spite. Even though they are always helping others and being nice, they often become the black sheep of the community, because they are so different and eccentric. They are the oddball family in the neighborhood, and it is very hard for them not to feel victimized. When confronted with a situation of great danger or stress, they usually show great vulnerability. They find difficulty coping and can end up in institutions, because the world is too harsh for them.

Bill had a grandmother who was sent by her family to a mental institution. Under her Girlchild myth was a lot of wisdom, and she could see through the family politics. One day, Bill said to Brian, "I was absolutely stunned! At the end of the Christmas holiday as Grandma was preparing to go back to the home, she said to me, 'You know, they are setting you up to sit in my place. I let them do it to me, because I really loved my family, and they needed to be boss. But do not let them do it to you. You do not want to live out your life as a stranger with strangers looking after you.'" Even though she appeared to be inept, she had seen through it all.

Father Family Myth (Extremely Rare)

Do you believe (but would never publicly admit) in a caste-like classification of people, where some are innately inferior because of their ethnicity, religion or socioeconomic status? Do you exercise enormous control over yourself emotionally in a public forum, but can you lose complete control in private? Do you thrill to have the public bend to your will, even if what you want is not truthful or right? Are you part of a social elite that politically and financially controls your local, state, national or international community? If so, you may have a Father social mask and family myth.

It seems that only a very small handful of people socialize through a Father archetype. The families that do so tend to work behind the scenes of government and society. They cultivate positions of complete social and political dominance. Examples of Unloving Father myth training are the rituals and initiations that some elite university fraternities and secret societies partake in, which are passed on from generation to generation.

People with a Father family myth are impersonal and usually play out the negative side of the Father archetype. The raw power and self-assurance that emanates from them can be hypnotic. They know how to get it so that others bend to their will. When they walk into a room, everyone tends to shrink back. They do not have to say a word to convince people that the world is their oyster.

✦

Assessing your family myth will help you to know which mask you socialize through and to understand how you behave in social situations. It will make you more aware of what your family values are and how these values impact the way your family relates to the outside world. As you study the strengths and weaknesses of your family myth and its corresponding archetype, you can start breaking self-limiting matrices that have been passed on—unquestioned—from generation to generation.

You can also start to experiment with all four loving archetypes in social situations, calling upon the Loving Mother's adultness, the Loving Father's impersonality, the Loved Boychild's enthusiasm or the Loved Girlchild's finesse to best respond to what is taking place around you. Your newfound flexibility will improve your social skills and your emotional intelligence (how you relate to others). It will help you become more authentic in the way you relate to others and see beyond the mask. Your children will take notice. They will model how to draw upon all four loving archetypes and, together, you can learn to transcend the limitations of your family myth.

Part Two ~ Key Concepts

There are five fundamental steps to self-knowledge. The first step is accessing your spiritual connection. The second step is understanding your thinking style. The third step is tapping your emotions. The fourth step is overcoming your sabotaging mechanism. The fifth step is identifying your social mask. Each of these steps reveals more of your ***personal archetypal pattern***.

Your ***personal archetypal pattern*** affects how you think, how you feel and how you relate to others. It also influences what kind of people you are drawn to and what kind of people you dislike.

The inner family archetype you aspire to is your ***spiritual archetype.*** It influences your spiritual connection and abides in your superconscious.

The inner family archetype you reason through is your ***thinking archetype.*** It impacts your reasoning ability and rules your conscious mind.

The inner family archetype you feel through is your ***feeling archetype.*** It determines your emotional reserve and dwells in your subconscious.

The inner family archetype you reject is your ***sabotaging archetype.*** It creates a sabotaging mechanism deep in your unconscious.

The inner family archetype through which you socialize is your *socialization archetype.* It describes your social mask. It will be the same as one of your four personal archetypes, and it will also apply to the rest of your family.

Your Archetypal Pattern

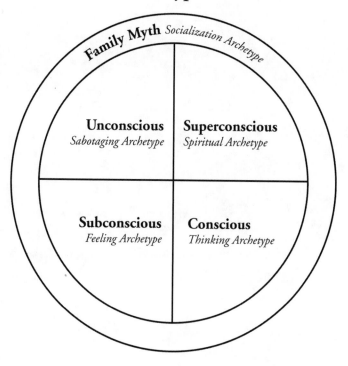

PART THREE

EIGHT PATTERNS
OF
BEHAVIOR

Our archetypal pattern of behavior helps us understand why we do what we do. It gives us our archetypal strengths and weaknesses. It shows us how our specific archetypes affect how authentic we are.

Our thinking and feeling archetypes reveal the most about us. They govern how we think and feel each day. They also identify how we can become split between the way we think (conscious archetype) and the way we feel (subconscious archetype.)

Our conscious and subconscious archetypes create eight primary archetypal patterns of behavior that people function through:

- The achievers (Conscious Boychild, subconscious Mother)
- The crusaders (Conscious Boychild, subconscious Girlchild)
- The stoics (Conscious Boychild, subconscious Father)
- The analysts (Conscious Mother, subconscious Boychild)
- The nurturers (Conscious Mother, subconscious Girlchild)
- The creators (Conscious Girlchild, subconscious Boychild)
- The inspirers (Conscious Girlchild, subconscious Mother)
- The overcomers (Conscious Girlchild, subconscious Father)

As you can see, none of these patterns place Father at the conscious level, because he does not naturally come up as a conscious archetype. You can also see that none of these patterns have two adult archetypes. When Father or Mother are subconsciously assigned,

Boychild or Girlchild rule the conscious mind. Mother can dominate at the conscious level so long as Boychild or Girlchild rules the subconscious. The more you work with all four loving archetypes and consciously express the qualities of the Loving Father and the Loving Mother, the more you can transcend the limitation of your specific pattern.

Your spiritual, superconscious and unconscious, sabotaging archetypes will influence your pattern of behavior, as will your socialization archetype. Therefore it is important to know what all of your archetypes are.

1. First, identify your conscious and subconscious archetypes.

Begin by identifying your conscious, thinking archetype. It is the one you are most familiar with, the one through which you think and function in your day-to-day affairs. Then assess your subconscious, feeling archetype. It is the one that governs your gut reactions and that best described you as a child.

(People who have conscious Girlchild can be harder to assess because Girlchild is like a chameleon. She can morph into different archetypal behaviors to respond to what other people want her to be. She tends to strongly play out her family myth and can appear to think through that archetype. Then, when she is offended, she often defers to her subconscious archetype and behaves like it.)

What is my conscious archetype (the one I think and function through most of the time) ?

_____

What is my subconscious archetype (the one I feel through, that best described me as a child) ?

_____

2. Then, identify your superconscious and unconscious archetypes.

To determine your superconscious, spiritual archetype, look at what archetype you would most like to be. (Some people mistakenly pick their superconscious archetype as their conscious archetype, because they so closely identify with what they aspire to be, so it is important to examine the two archetypes with care.) Then, find your unconscious, sabotaging archetype by figuring out what archetypal behavior irritates you the most.

What is my superconscious archetype (the one I aspire to most) ?

_____

What is my unconscious archetype (the one that I find most repelling) ?

_____

Note: As you assess your four personal archetypes (spiritual, thinking, feeling, sabotaging) remember that the same archetype cannot be assigned to two levels of self simultaneously. You cannot, for instance, have a dominant Boychild archetype in the superconscious and a dominant Boychild archetype in the subconscious. If you intuit that you have a conscious Boychild and a subconscious Mother archetype, your superconscious and unconscious dominant archetypes would have to be Girlchild and Father, or vice versa.

3. Finish by identifying your socialization archetype.

Your socialization archetype describes your family myth—the social training you inherited. It needs to fit your family as well as yourself.

Which archetype describes how I was taught to socialize (and also fits my family) ?

_____

Note: Your socialization archetype is not a personal archetype. It applies to other family members as well. It is a filter through which your four personal archetypes express themselves, and it will be the same as one of your four personal archetypes. In our experience, Boychild is the most common socialization archetype, followed by Mother. Girlchild is a rare socialization archetype and Father is extremely rare.

Part Three describes each of the eight patterns of behavior and how they mesh with the superconscious, unconscious and family myth archetypes. You will find a childhood description for each pattern, along with an explanation of the archetypal shift that happens at puberty. As you study the information, remember that the challenges experienced in childhood, which are reflected through the subconscious archetype, are general descriptions. Everyone's childhood is different and some children experience more pain than others.

The more you study these patterns, the more you will be able to recognize the ones that most appropriately fit you and your loved ones. Eventually, you can recognize the archetypal pattern of friends, coworkers, people you have just met and even public figures. The knowledge will provide you with an understanding of others that can help you make the most of all of your relationships.

If you recognize yourself or someone else in the following section, keep in mind that you are observing general patterns of behavior and that people always express their archetypes in a unique way. In each chapter, you will also find examples of celebrities that seem to express a specific archetypal pattern in their public life. Again, these assessments are not meant to judge, criticize or limit anyone. They are only intended to illustrate a general archetypal pattern of behavior.

Ten

The Achievers

All mankind is divided into three classes:
those that are immovable, those that are movable,
and those that move.
—Benjamin Franklin

People who have a dominant conscious Boychild and subconscious Mother (Boy-Mother) pattern are achievers. They are movers and shakers in life, those who get things done. They are self-sufficient, can accomplish just about anything and tend to have their way with the world.

Boychild feels nurtured by Mother and thinks he's on top of things. His mental sharpness, action and aggressive will to discover is backed by her innate wisdom, nurturance, and expansiveness, which provide him with all the information he needs to carry out his plan. A strong emotional maturity comes out automatically and gives him the wherewithal to be successful.

Boy-Mothers are very popular and people tend to congregate around them. Conscious Boychild dominates the room by the shininess in his eyes and the sheer excitement that emanates from him. He does not see anything lacking in himself and sets out to fill all the gaps outside of himself. He is always checking, "Who can benefit from my presence now?"

Boy-Mothers are also good leaders in a time of crisis. There was a mayor in a televised meeting during an earthquake who appeared to have a Boy-Mother pattern of behavior. In that moment, she dropped into her subconscious Mother fall-back position and became very composed. Calmly she said, "I think that the time has come for us to get under our desks." Everybody obliged, responding to her innate adultness.

Former British Prime Minister Margaret Thatcher outpictured this Boy-Mother poise time and time again during her years of service. Her emotional reserve and her willingness to take action against all odds gained the respect of many in the international community. She was the iron lady, known as someone who could get things done and would stand up to anyone when necessary.

Boy-Mothers lean on the arm of objective reality, which is their place of strength, and are often drawn to athletics. They tend not to get involved in artistic pursuits, and would rather have Mother Nature expose her special gifts to them through science. In so doing, they search for resolution with their own subconscious Mother.

Their greatest strength lies in discovering how things work and then putting them into a form that everyone else can understand. When you are in a group of people, you can tell who the Boy-Mothers are, because they explain the wisdom and delineate the philosophy of what they happen to be working with. In a school setting, they are usually the heads of the faculty, the heads of the class or those who graduate Summa Cum Laude and go on to re-create the system. Most people feel inferior to them, because they are so smooth, quick and competent.

Boy-Mothers also know what attracts people subconsciously, which makes them excellent in sales and marketing, where they can easily get others to appreciate a concept or a product. Bill Gates is a good example of a Boy-Mother who knows exactly what people want and can deliver it. He always seeks to maintain a Boychild competitive edge that allows him to stay ahead of the game, and that he defends by being emotionally aloof to negative feedback.

Boy-Mothers tend to keep such tight control over their own mind that they believe it gives them the right to control others. They often gravitate towards situations where they can be in charge, like law enforcement. Actor Don Johnson portrays this Boy-Mother energy in his roles as the tough, no-nonsense cop, who always charms the women. His subconscious Mother helps him to stay emotionally mature while his conscious Boychild investigates, takes action and charms his way into nailing the "bad guy" and restoring justice.

General MacArthur, who was in charge of the Pacific front during World War II, was also a Boy-Mother. The perseverance of his Loved Boychild, combined with the organizational strength of his Loving Mother, allowed him to lead the charge against the entire Japanese fleet until their capitulation. Then, he was sent into the Korean conflict, where he would have done away with communist aggression had he not been provoked and covertly sabotaged by the powers-that-be.

Boy-Mothers tend to rebel against that which they cannot taste, touch or see. They are usually not attracted towards mystical, New Age or unorthodox groups unless they are born into them. They generally do not seek out personal counseling or group therapy, because they tend not to find anything wrong with themselves.

Boy-Mothers are often driven by emotional aloofness. This can be a good thing. Like a surgeon, it gives them the ability to dissect a situation from stem to stern without thinking twice about it. It can also turn Boy-Mothers into bullies who have no scruples, because they are aloof to outside feedback. They can use people—and when the other person's use runs out, the relationship is over. Boy-Mothers must ultimately learn that for their plans to work out, they must stop running over the people who will carry out those plans for them.

Brian's grandfather was a Boy-Mother. One day, when Brian was 21 years old, he said to Brian, "You're going to take over the farm. You'll need money and your own farming equipment. I'm going to show you how to do it."

They headed to town and Grandpa breezed into the bank manager's office, ignoring the tellers who tried to stop them. The manager looked up at them from his work.

"Hey Jo," said Grandpa. "How's your boy doing, your oldest boy?"

"Well, he's doing real well," he replied, wondering what Grandpa had up his sleeve.

"You remember, Jo, when you brought me the boy that summer and you said that he needed to be made a man? Did I give you back a man, Jo?"

"Well, yeah, sure. You did really well."

"Now, how much does he make every year?"

Jo's face was getting a little pale, because he knew Grandpa was in predator mode and was calling in the tickets.

"He makes a lot," he said.

"Sure he makes a lot," said Grandpa. "I got my boy here, he needs to get a tractor, a cultivator, a combine... all the equipment."

Brian walked out of the bank at 21 years of age with a $25,000 loan and no co-signer or collateral. Then, they pushed their way from implement dealership to implement dealership and got $55,000 worth of equipment. Finally, Grandpa bullied an assessor to assess the equipment at a higher rate and they came back to the bank manager's office.

"Jo," Grandpa said. "We spent the $25,000 that you lent the boy here, and we just made you $30,000. Now we want that, sir, in cash." By the end of the day, Brian had all the farming equipment he needed, a truck, and a $30,000 line of credit.

Boy-Mothers know how to get their way, and the world acclimatizes itself to them. One Fourth of July, Therese went out with almost thirty people to a small restaurant in a little town. Even though it was the end of a long, busy day, the kitchen staff set up tables and chairs in a back room. The young waitress was trying her Girlchild best to meet everyone's needs. She started walking around the three long tables to take orders and figure out whose check went with whose order. The menu was sparse. The only vegetables advertised were frozen French fries and onion rings.

She worked her way to Frank—a Boy-Mother type—who said, "I'll have a vegetarian special."

"We do not have a vegetarian special," she explained.

"Yes, you do," he replied.

"What do you mean?" she stammered, confused. Frank was exuding Boy-Mother confidence and had her convinced that he knew the menu better than she did.

"Look, you must have some vegetables in the kitchen, onion, carrots, broccoli—just ask the chef to put them in a skillet. Cook them with some olive oil, add salt and a little soy sauce. Then get some rice, any rice. You must have rice pilaf." He completed the recipe with "You tell the chef it has to be cooked *this* fast to achieve *this* texture" direction. Then he smiled. "That's your vegetarian special!" he said. "It will be $6.95. Oh, and you see that girl over there?" pointing to one of his friends in the group. "She'll have one too."

Thirty pairs of eyes were staring at him, incredulously. Needless, to say, he had the best meal of anyone there. The price he set was never questioned and he left completely satisfied, suggesting that everyone do it his way next time. He did not have a clue that he had imposed in any way on the group, the chef or on the waitress.

Boy-Mothers can be the most formidable adversaries. When they behave their worst, they let people know, "I can get my way before you get yours, and I will not think twice about it. I can tear off your family myth mask, find your weakest point and go for it." The people they run over respond by feeling vulnerable, victimized and ultimately superior—I would never behave *this* way, they think!

Boy-Mothers want to feel connected to others, but they are often hampered by their emotional aloofness. They prefer to dominate a situation superficially than to give of themselves in an authentic way. If someone they are close to shares something too personal, they may tune out and wonder, "Why is this person telling me all these details?"

They ever so much want to experience closeness with others, but when their Unloved Boychild takes over, they release aggressiveness and then become aloof to the fact that they did so. They tend to fill their void for intimacy by convincing others of the right path to follow, or by competing and battling with them. After all, is there anything more intimate than someone you are fighting or competing with?

It is important to be inclusive of Boy-Mothers and to give them attention and nurturing so they can resolve the abandonment they experienced at an early age. If we can avoid taking offense when their Unloved Boychild seeks to dominate and stay impersonal, we will win their trust, friendship and loyalty.

Boy-Mothers bear incredible gifts, talents and abilities, and we do not want to cut ourselves off from them. We must simply remember that they are used to getting their way in life and do not want to give that up. Before criticizing them, we must consider that if we were in their shoes, we would probably behave the same way.

If we tell them they are behaving negatively with the intent to scold them, they will not change. If we show them we are earnestly trying to be helpful, they will listen and take note. It is important to address them with the Loving Father. "You know, what you did with that girl was to tell her what her job was. You made her feel insignificant—that no matter what she did, there was nothing she could do that was right."

Boy-Mothers can improve their relationships by delving deep into their subconscious ability to nurture life. With the help of the Loving Father, they can curb conscious Boychild's compulsive need to be in charge and offer a cup of motherly care to others. The more they learn to put other people's needs before their own, the more they will attract the quality of relationship they secretly yearn for.

From Childhood to Adulthood

As little children, Boy-Mothers were forced to operate from an adult archetype. Their parents trained them to behave in a mature way to avoid expending energy looking after them. Having subconscious Mother usually indicates that it may have been necessary for them to nurture one of their parents instead of the other way around. This may have left them feeling abandoned subconsciously.

When they enter puberty and their Boychild side comes out, they may balk against this lack of nurturing and respond aggressively to the person who was supposed to mother the family. "That's it," they decide. "I'm going to get the attention not only of my parents but of the whole town." This happened to Patty, who became so rebellious as she moved from subconscious Mother to Boychild, that she says her parents had to ground her to the kitchen for four years.

Eventually, the situation turns in Boy-Mother's favor. Action and dexterity emerge, reinforced by their subconscious platform of wisdom and maturity. Overall, the transition from Mother to Boychild is a good transition, and Boy-Mothers tend to have a shining moment in high school. They are usually very popular in school and have an extra charm about them. They are excellent at sports and team leadership and often end up as class president. The support they receive from their peers establishes a base of self-confidence in social situations that will serve them for the rest of their lives.

Superconscious and Unconscious Archetypes

Boy-Mothers can either have a superconscious Father and unconscious Girlchild archetype or vice-versa. Finding the placement of these two archetypes offers greater insight into their behavior.

Boy-Mother with Superconscious Father and Unconscious Girlchild

Superconscious	Father
Conscious	**Boychild**
Subconscious	**Mother**
Unconscious	Girlchild

Boy-Mothers with superconscious Father and unconscious Girlchild appreciate structure and have no problem following rules. They seek to uphold the law in their affairs and to pull down their superconscious Father connection. Unfortunately, they have been trained to give away their spiritual connection and reject Girlchild. They also tend to have no regard for people who think in a spherical way and do not fit into their linear perspective.

People with this archetypal pattern have a nice, strong flow of energy. They tend to believe that they can do whatever they set their mind to and often volunteer for projects. Even though they appear to be very contained, they can still be emotionally nurturing. They approach situations from a "we, our, us" methodological standpoint and can really get in and take things apart.

Many are scientists, like Isaac Newton. They focus the "can-do" spirit of Boychild and the wisdom of Mother. Boychild seeks to bring forth the laws of Father in a sterile environment where he can consistently reproduce his results without Girlchild unpredictability.

In everyday life, these individuals are usually very successful. The only drawback is that because they exclude Girlchild, they may end up attracting hostility from Girlchild-types who feel put down by them and then overtly or covertly seek to tear them down.

Boy-Mother with Superconscious Girlchild and Unconscious Father

Superconscious	Girlchild
Conscious	*Boychild*
Subconscious	*Mother*
Unconscious	Father

Boy-Mothers with superconscious Girlchild and unconscious Father are quite different. Because Girlchild is in their superconscious, they do not reject her. Instead, they seek to defend her in their relationships with others. They also aspire to Girlchild through a Boy-Mother scientific frame of reference and become inventors. They look for the magic in things and are often on the cutting edge of science. They are always trying to draw from what Plato called the "realm of ideals" and see Girlchild as guardian of that realm.

They can be a little wacky in their discoveries, because they are trying to capture spirit and break the mold to discover the non-linear, spherical side of life. They must learn to be more impersonal as they search the secrets of the universe. They must also resist the temptation to make data conform to their search. This was seen in the physics debate that took place between scientists who had discovered that light was formed of particles and scientists who had discovered that light was formed of waves. Neither side wanted to give up their interpretation of the data. In the end, both sides were right.

Boy-Mothers with Father in the unconscious like to prove that rules do not apply. They also need to guard against unconscious criticism and a bulldozer mentality that would destroy the Girlchild treasures they seek. Overall, they can be very successful, as long as they refrain from releasing their unconscious criticism on others.

Family Myths

Just as Boy-Mothers are influenced by their superconscious and unconscious archetypal pattern, so they are influenced by their socialization archetype.

Boy-Mother with a Boychild Family Myth (Most Common)

Boychild Family Myth	Conscious Boychild
	Subconscious Mother

Boy-Mothers with a Boychild myth are especially good at selling ideas, and they sometimes manipulate people in the process. They can display a lot of aloofness and can also be very invasive. They may have a hard time socializing. They do not know how to get their point across without being pushy and turning people off. Then, they get angry about being rejected and abandoned. If someone, for example, does not return their persistent phone calls, they take offense.

These Boy-Mothers must especially focus on bringing up subconscious Loving Mother's nurturance in their relationships. When they do so, they will override their excessive Boychild zeal and begin to create authentic relationships with others.

Boy-Mother with a Mother Family Myth (Common)

Mother Family Myth	Conscious Boychild
	Subconscious Mother

Boy-Mothers with a Mother family myth can be very successful in social situations. They know how to communicate in a way that holds other people's interest and attention. Their motherly energy and adult behavior also makes others feel safe to open up in their presence. Conscious Boychild, however, may want to capitalize on the information and goodwill that others volunteer for his *own* gain. In order to keep the trust of a group, these Boy-Mothers must refrain from giving into any Boychild scheming.

Boy-Mother with a Girlchild Family Myth (Rare)

Girlchild Family Myth	Conscious Boychild
	Subconscious Mother

Boy-Mothers with a Girlchild family myth displayed a lot of maturity as children, even though they were raised in a difficult family situation and may have been ostracized in their community. They likely experienced many put-downs in school from ridicule directed at their family.

These Boy-Mothers learn to overcome the injury by taking care of others who are still less fortunate than they are. By doing so, they gain the strength, the self-esteem and the respect that eluded them as children.

Boy-Mother with a Father Family Myth (Extremely Rare)

Father	Conscious Boychild
Family	
Myth	Subconscious Mother

Boy-Mothers who socialize through a Father archetype would use the power of Father to capture the admiration of their circle of influence and feed upon the breast of that collective. The problem is that, eventually, other people would resent Unloving Father's need to dominate, and turn on him, triggering this type's subconscious Mother fear of abandonment. The more Boy-Mothers would aspire to socialize through the Loving Father, the more impervious they would become to the swing of public opinion, as they channel their energy into principle-based, rather than personality-based leadership. An example of this is the scientist who is willing, like Copernicus, to put his status on the line in order to promote a great, albeit controversial discovery—that the earth is not the center of the universe, and orbits around the sun.

Boy-Mothers at a Glance

- ◆ Boy-Mothers are achievers who get things done.

- ◆ They lean on the arm of objective reality.

- ◆ They are smooth, quick and competent.

- ◆ They want to be in charge and they can be pushy.

- ◆ They are very popular, and people tend to congregate around them.

- ◆ They often get involved in athletics, scientific fields, investigative endeavors or promotional work.

Eleven

The Crusaders

Nothing great in the world
has ever been accomplished without passion.
—Georg Hegel

People who have a conscious Boychild and subconscious Girlchild (Boy-Girl) pattern are very energetic and extremely creative. They can work miracles. They can sell ice cubes to Eskimos. They are good writers and storytellers and have a wonderful stage presence about them. With their double-child drama, sensitivity, charm and sense of humor, they can access a gamut of emotions to make their audience laugh, cry or rally together.

Many Hollywood actors seem to have this pattern—Elizabeth Taylor, Mel Gibson, Keanu Reeves, Drew Barrymore, Tom Cruise, Bruce Willis and Julia Roberts to name a few. Under their dynamic, creative, adventurous, gutsy and charming Boychild presence lies a soft spot, their Girlchild's care and sensitivity.

Boy-Girls also have an ongoing desire to rescue seemingly lost causes, so that Boychild can be a champion and Girlchild can save the seemingly unsavable. This is the shepherd mechanism. Their greatest love is to take something in an underdog position and raise it up, be it a person or a cause. This dedication is evident in Mel Gibson's film, *The Passion of the Christ.*

Oprah Winfrey is another good role model of the Loved Boychild shepherd, who seeks to champion righteousness by bringing that which is in darkness to light. Her conscious Boychild facilitates the caring of her subconscious Girlchild, and she seeks to illumine all to the problems that are created when people and society avoid personal giving and personal responsibility. She has earned her stripes by transcending difficult personal circumstances against all odds. She is an example of someone who works to unfold all four loving archetypes at the conscious level by continuously striving to overcome her limitations. That is her magic.

Boy-Girls are extremely motivated and earnest. Even though most Boy-Girls want to be in charge, they will easily give their authority and leadership to another, so long as the person in charge stays in line. But if their leader abuses power in any way, it becomes very difficult to keep their support.

Boy-Girls will work day and night for you as long as you treat them right and as long as they feel the cause you are working for is righteous. When they are on your team and functioning at their best, they will do a good job every time. Their loyalty and dedication can really pull things off. The challenge they bring to others is that they tend to behave in an all-or-nothing way and want things done yesterday. They become easily bored and need continuous stimulation to keep their attention focused and their interest from fading.

The television show *I Love Lucy* illustrates the Boy-Girl personality taken to an extreme. No one is bored around Lucy. She is bubbly, enthusiastic and cannot sit still for a minute. Her life is full of surprises that provide meaning for her. Every unexpected twist offers a new challenge and opportunity for her to leave her creative mark on the events and people that come into her life. Lucy has no compunction managing other people's lives, because she has good intentions. She continually sets out to prove that her way is right in every imaginable, far-out situation.

Subconscious Girlchild genuinely cares for others and wants to convert them to a better place. Meanwhile, conscious Boychild wants people to rally around him, following his lead. Lucy's Boychild takes the lead in such a boisterous way that it becomes humorous. He gets so excited about whatever new cause, whim or agenda he has drummed up to convert people to a better place that he cannot slow down. He wants to save people, usually in spite of themselves, and when he does not get his way, subconscious Girlchild pouts.

Boy-Girls love crusades and want everybody to see as they see, to believe as they believe, to like what they like and to join their happy team under their direction. Television personality, Frasier, is another wonderful example of this pattern. Like Lucy before him, Frasier makes America laugh each night by playing out Boy-Girl's psychology to excess.

Frasier is a psychologist who hosts a Seattle radio talk show. He lives to tell people how to improve their lives by following his directives. Even though he cares about his listeners, what he cares most about is his Boychild ego, which gets easily ruffled and sends his Girlchild sulking in self-reflecting misery.

Like all Boy-Girls, Frasier is most thrilled when he succeeds in getting others to follow in his footsteps. In one episode, for instance, Frasier revels in the fact that his new boss asks him to be his mentor in how to dress, eat, decorate his apartment and live in style—until things take an unexpected turn. Any circumstance where others do not acquiesce to his better judgment sends a devastating, albeit humorous, blow to his ego, which keeps his audience laughing. Eventually, he always comes around through a grumpy process of self-realization, which forces him to practice the enlightenment that he preaches on his radio show.

Boy-Girls live to bring their realizations into the world. They can be fiery preachers and evangelists. Like anyone with a strong Girlchild archetype, they are often very much in touch with heaven. Boychild knows how to capture the moment and Girlchild knows how to access the Holy Spirit. Foursquare Gospel evangelist, Aimee Semple McPherson, is a classic example of a Boy-Girl type who took America by storm in the 1930s, converting thousands with her dramatic Boychild stage presence and her subconscious welling up of Holy Spirit energy.

Boy-Girls can also make people uncomfortable because they are like a wild card that cannot be controlled. Take the classic story of *The Emperor's New Clothes*[*]. People are sitting in the emperor's court. The emperor is getting ready to be dressed, but his fine Chinese silk robe is lost, and the courtiers know their heads are going to roll. They open a fancy box and pull out a shimmering, sheer robe that only an emperor could wear. "Is not it delicate?" they tell him. "You cannot even feel your arm going into the sleeve."

"Yes, yes, it is fabulous," he says and he walks up to his throne. "My wonderful new robe," he says to the crowd. "The finest silk, you can barely see it." Everyone knows there's no robe but they cheer anyway. Only the Boy-Girl in the front row shouts, "Hey, the emperor has no clothes!"

---

[*] Written by Hans Christian Andersen

With their double child energy, Boy-Girls lack a certain adult composure and can become untethered like a helium balloon. As a result, many people criticize them as unstable and they, in turn, tend to criticize themselves. Boychild is always searching for hints of criticism in the face of whomever he talks to or happens to walk by. He picks up strong visual cues, like other people's body language, to determine where he stands in the game. Meanwhile, Girlchild extends an antenna, a hyper-sensitive radar, that can sense criticism two hundred and fifty yards away.

Relationships with Boy-Girls can be wonderful, but if they go sour, things can get very ugly. When this happens, it is best not to take the situation personally and understand that the china of Boy-Girls' sensitivity was knocked over, setting off an alarm. Even if the Boy-Girls were not personally offended, someone or something they were in support of was, which detonated their subconscious Girlchild victim pattern.

Boy-Girls wear their feelings on their coat sleeve. You never have to ask them, "Gee, how are you feeling today?" because it is obvious. They often succumb to an aggressive victim pattern. Girlchild gets hurt or upset about something: "You did this to me!" And Boychild becomes aggressive to rectify the situation. Any time Girlchild feels victimized, Boychild believes he has every right to control others through whatever aggressive tactic that is necessary.

Boy-Girls' sense of victimization, deeply registered in the subconscious, is always anchored in a past injury that was very real. It is never a random, perchance reaction. When we work with a Boy-Girl, we need to remember that their aggressive victim pattern is not personally directed at us but rather at those who first injured them. If we say, "That person's a jerk," we only further confirm their grievance.

When Boy-Girls are not hurt by someone externally, they tend to persecute themselves. In this case, Boychild denigrates subconscious Girlchild, because he thinks she makes him gutless and hampers his success with her willy-nilly ways (even though it is never really so). Boychild moves quickly, with lightning and thunder, and ends up dragging Girlchild behind him in the mud when she cannot keep up. He wants to be the only champion and cannot let Girlchild shine, because that would be competition. If by accident she expresses herself in a way that looks good, he tends to take credit for her accomplishments.

In order to help Boy-Girls, we need to be adult and see them for who they are, beyond their aggressive victim pattern. It is crucial for us to understand that the double-child types dwell in the moment more than anyone else. Like a painter who gets lost in his canvas, Boy-Girls tend to get lost in the moment. A moment, for them, turns into eternity. When the moment is beautiful, they are transported and enthralled. When it is bad, Boychild rebels. He does not want that moment and somebody's got to pay. In joyful events, Boy-Girls beam with light. When life disappoints them, they become lead-heavy and toxic. Boychild will revolve the offending situation over and over in an attempt to gain control, which only further prolongs the agony.

Boy-Girls must learn to distance themselves from the immediate now. When things seem unbearable, we can remind them, "This is how it is right now. This is not necessarily how it will be ten minutes from now." We can provide them with Loving Mother explanations, teaching their Boychild which way to go and reassuring their Girlchild of her worth.

It is important for Boy-Girls to know that we are there for them, that we hear what they are saying and that we are not denying them or what they are saying.

Otherwise, we may break their trust and, once that trust is broken, it is very difficult to get back. To keep their trust, we must always go the extra mile and let them know what we are about and what our intentions are.

The minute we tell Boy-Girls how to transcend their negative pattern, they get very excited and want to heroically do it right away. The only problem is that when, in good intention, they bite off more than they can chew, they tend to blame the other person. If Boy-Girls are willing to persist, to unfold the adult presence of their superconscious archetype and not give in to their childish aggressive victim pattern, they can, in time, succeed in building solid and fulfilling relationships with people who will appreciate all of the talent and goodwill they bring to the world.

From Childhood to Adulthood

People who have subconscious Girlchild often experience some kind of abandonment, lack of nurturing or aggression in childhood. Later in life, they tend to compensate by becoming addicted to eating, shopping, working, relationships, sex, alcohol or drugs—anything that will satisfy their subconscious urge for Mother attention.

As they transit to Boychild, this type becomes more aggressive to gain control over their lives. Their Boychild starts to figure out that every time Girlchild comes out, people either are very sweet to them or take advantage of them. Then they begin to treat people accordingly. Those who favor them receive consideration and amiability; those who do not are met with aggression and control.

The transition from Girlchild to Boychild is not always unpleasant, because they shed their vulnerability and become more dexterous in social situations. Sometimes the shift can be extreme—from a contained, docile child to an overactive, off-the-wall teenager who engages in all kinds of wild and crazy activities. If the behavior draws more alienation than approval from their peers, Girlchild suffers and Boychild compensates by rebelling even more. A good mentor or source of inspiration can help Boy-Girls weather this storm and develop the depth of character they will be able to draw from for the rest of their life.

Superconscious and Unconscious Archetypes

Boy-Girls have double-child primary archetypes, so it is especially important for them to access the adult qualities of their superconscious and unconscious archetypes. They can either have a superconscious Father and an unconscious Mother placement or vice-versa. Finding the placement of these two archetypes offers greater insight into their behavior.

Boy-Girl with Superconscious Father and Unconscious Mother

Superconscious	Father
Conscious	**Boychild**
Subconscious	**Girlchild**
Unconscious	Mother

Boy-Girls with superconscious Father and unconscious Mother are very inspired and can stay focused as they receive that inspiration. When they center on the wisdom in their hearts, they can pull down the superconscious blueprint of what is to come through their connection with superconscious Father.

They revel in discipline and can be quite blunt. They look to God as a strict, disciplinarian energy or figure and often tie themselves to powerful people, who represent the law for them. Their rejection of unconscious Mother makes it difficult for them to be truly personal with people, even though they might appear that way in a public forum. In private, they tend to reject anyone or anything too personal that comes to them, which deprives them of the feedback they need to succeed. When they learn to reconcile with the Loving Mother, they will be able to open up to intimate exchanges with others and benefit from those relationships.

Boy-Girl with Superconscious Mother and Unconscious Father

Superconscious	Mother
Conscious	**Boychild**
Subconscious	**Girlchild**
Unconscious	Father

Boy-Girls with superconscious Mother and unconscious Father derive their greatest joy from attaining Loving Mother's wisdom. They tune into the "who, what, where, when and why" of things and convert others to their inspiration. They look to God as a wonderful, all-encompassing, unconditional love and seek intimacy from that perspective.

Father in the unconscious makes them unorthodox and more rebellious. They are always avoiding the law and have a hard time functioning within a strong parameter of expectations and rules. Sometimes, they take up issue with superconscious Loving Mother, who tells them, "We have to obey Loving Father's rules, if we are to be successful."

When someone reflects their superconscious archetype—nurturing, guiding and loving them unconditionally, their allegiance is eternal. If, however, somebody embodies their unconscious archetype and becomes even a little critical of them or imposes strong rules upon them, they become hypersensitive and tend to overreact, until they learn to become more impersonal.

People with this pattern must come to peace with the Loving Father, because they need him to protect their creativity from other people's criticism. The Loving Father will help them create a healthy definition of self. Otherwise, they will be defined by others, who will not take the time to appreciate who they are or the gifts that they bring.

Family Myths

Just as Boy-Girls are influenced by their superconscious and unconscious archetypal pattern, so they are influenced by their socialization archetype.

Boy-Girl with a Boychild Family Myth (Most Common)

Boychild	Conscious Boychild
Family	
Myth	Subconscious Girlchild

Boy-Girls with a Boychild family myth are extremely creative. They have been taught to interface through Boychild in a tough way, but the energy they project comes back to land on their subconscious Girlchild sensitivity.

Like all Boy-Girls, they are hyper-vigilant about being victimized and criticized and become aggressive when that happens. With a Boychild myth, they have even less compunction about how they react. Because of this, they end up having trouble in social situations. They are often put down by authority figures within a group, for example, because they do not have the adult reserve to be quiet about what they have seen. When they speak out loudly against what they consider wrong, the authority who is looking to maintain the status quo one way or the other exiles them from the group by telling them that they are wacky, unpredictable or rabble-rousing. To survive, these Boy-Girls need to learn to resist the urge to blurt everything that would come out of their mouths, because they tend to offend others in spite of themselves.

Bridget Jones, in the 2001 hit comedy, *Bridget Jones's Diary*, is a typical example of a Boy-Girl with a Boychild myth. She cannot seem to hold back, neither in life nor in her diary. Her fresh honesty and childlike spontaneity won the hearts of audiences around the world, and the blunders she makes are entertaining to watch. In real life, though, the challenges Boy-Girls with a Boychild myth often face as they interact with others can be much harder to deal with than on the screen.

To resolve their tendency for making social faux pas, Boy-Girls with a Boychild myth must strive to consciously hone the loving qualities of their superconscious and unconscious adult archetypes without crunching their child self or sacrificing their creativity.

Boy-Girl with a Mother Family Myth (Common)

Mother Family Myth	Conscious Boychild
	Subconscious Girlchild

Boy-Girls who have a Mother myth are much more sophisticated in social situations and can move into a position of prestige. They also tend to bend to authority rather than resist it. Unlike Boy-Girls with a Boychild myth, they know how to be diplomatic, because they have the ability to interface in an adult way. They can be great teachers and are always looking for an audience that will honor their message.

When they were children, they interpreted their family aloofness as a criticism of their Girlchild and responded by downplaying her presence. As adults, they continue to disown their Girlchild to avoid appearing weak. This makes them less sensitive to other people's needs and less aware of when they hurt others' feelings. Still, this strategy does not preclude aggressive behavior from others, who eventually detect their hidden Girlchild vulnerability.

Nevertheless, their Mother myth is a blessing that allows them to be composed and adult around other people, to be shock absorbers in difficult situations and to hold a group together.

Boy-Girl with a Girlchild Family Myth (Rare)

Girlchild	Conscious Boychild
Family	
Myth	Subconscious Girlchild

Boy-Girls with a Girlchild family myth learn to deal with enormous chaos in their lives. They tend to be put down by others and labeled as odd people. From the time they were teenagers, they decided there was no way to fight the oddness of their family myth, so they played it out, sometimes to extremes. It is as if their conscious Boychild were saying, "If we're going to be looked upon as weird, we're going to show you what weird is."

On a positive note, they can really tune in to other people's needs and transfer their creativity and spiritual connection to others. They also have the potential to be gifted artists like Van Gogh, but they must learn to resist the urge to mail their ear to would-be girlfriends!

Boy-Girl with a Father Family Myth (Extremely Rare)

Father	Conscious Boychild
Family	
Myth	Subconscious Girlchild

Conscious Boychild and subconscious Girlchild is a creative combination with enormous potential that can be used for good or for ill. A Father socialization pattern would only amplify this potential. With Unloving Father, Boy-Girls would have an extreme need to dominate others in order to stifle any perceived criticism of their Girlchild. With a Loving Father code of conduct, they would feel completely safe to launch their inspiration and perform great works. An example of Boy-Girl creativity protected by Loving Father parameters is that of Russian painter, Nicholas Roerich, who established an international treaty to safeguard works of art and sites of cultural and historical interest from the ravages of war.

Boy-Girls at a Glance

◆ Boy-Girls are very energetic and extremely creative.

◆ They are always looking to help the underdog and love crusades.

◆ Their loyalty and dedication pulls things off, but they tend to be all-or-nothing and want everything done right away.

◆ They are not easily controlled. Others may put them down as being unstable, while still making use of their talents.

◆ Boy-Girls wear their feelings on their coat sleeve and sometimes succumb to an aggressive victim pattern.

◆ They tend to dwell in the moment.

Twelve

The Stoics

Valor is stability, not of legs and arms,
but of courage and the soul.
—Michel de Montaigne

People with a dominant conscious Boychild and subconscious Father (Boy-Father) pattern are rare, and their pattern merits more study. They have active, can-do energy at the conscious level, coupled with a forceful directive pattern in the subconscious. This can be difficult to manage, especially in women.

Boy-Fathers can conquer extreme challenges and often end up in military or law enforcement work, where guns are involved. They display power combined with action. They are very rough-and-ready and know how to get the job done. They seek to find out how everything works and can take things apart with great detachment.

Boy-Fathers have a lot of personal magnetism and look very bright and shiny to others, but behind their social front, we find a pillar of iron impersonality. People can get along with them extremely well, because they do not seem to carry a lot of emotional baggage. They are stoic, take things as they come and think that whatever is happening to them is just the way things are.

Those who have this archetypal combination can also be politically savvy, as in the case of Governor of

California Arnold Shwarzenegger. And yet even if they have an enormous desire to lead the pack, they are also willing to be good followers, when the situation requires.

Boy-Fathers are great heroes in any crisis. They are the survivors who help others out of difficult situations. They can see beyond the "groupthink" and usually do not land in the same trap as everyone else. When push comes to shove and everybody's in a panic because the room is on fire and the emergency door won't open, they calmly work things out and remember to push the right button.

Boy-Fathers shine in the thick of the fight, but much like Winston Churchill, they sometimes feel as if they have no place to go when the battle is over. During World War II, Churchill was irreplaceable for the defense of England, but once peacetime came, he was voted out by the very people whose lives he had championed in their darkest hour.

Boy-Fathers can shoot themselves in the foot, because they lack emotional intelligence. They have no primary feminine archetypes and need to cultivate wisdom (Loving Mother) and caring (Loved Girlchild). Instead, they often prefer to lean toward orthodoxy, toward hard and fast rules that are empirically obvious, and frown upon Girlchild intuition. They are more accepting of Mother, because they know she is an inventory of data they can use but do not always respect her.

When Boy-Fathers do not take into account the impact their words, feelings, actions and agendas have on the people around them, they shut down their feedback loop and make costly mistakes, even though they believe they are only calling a spade a spade.

Caroline knows a Boy-Father who runs a company. He has little sympathy for himself or others, and his subconscious Father gives him a towering perfectionist urge that he has to live up to, no matter what. When he comes into contact with somebody who is tired, forgot something or made a mistake, he cannot fathom it. After all, how could anyone possibly want a day off?

Boy-Fathers' drive for perfection can destroy group morale and end up in mediocrity. If they treat people as paid robots, they may achieve mechanical perfection but will never experience creative transcendence.

Part of the reason Boy-Fathers have such a tough underbelly is that they usually come from families where personal care and intimacy was supplanted by rules. Their early childhood training was very demanding, almost military-like, and they often treat others like they were treated. When someone appears weak, they wonder what is wrong with that person.

They tend to forget how difficult things really were during their early years and live to prove that they have no affliction. The chance of finding a Boy-Father in a self-help therapy group or a counseling session, where they might be analyzed or assessed, is very slim. The message they send is that life is great and that they have no problems. This can be very attractive to others and greatly enhances their public image. Nevertheless, despite all appearances, Boy-Fathers tend to suffer from a deep subconscious pattern of self-criticism that was generated in childhood.

Self-criticism is a great vulnerability. It leads Boy-Fathers to shoot themselves in the foot by criticizing others with the same level of criticism they reserve for themselves. Oftentimes, they can get pulled into very difficult, abusive relationships that go on for years. They are used to toughing it out and become desensitized. They may think it is normal to relate like that or think they deserve to be treated harshly.

Boy-Fathers put up with a lot, but when someone gets on their bad side, they may "erase" that person out of their lives just like they erased their own childhood pain. Once you have been erased, they will not acknowledge your presence, even if you greet them in a doorway.

Boy-Fathers' subconscious self-criticism can sabotage their ability to lead others. Every group subconsciously hunts for the leader's weakness. In the case of Boy-Father, when the honeymoon is over, the collective subconscious starts to hone in on Boy-Father's weak link, especially when conscious Boychild forgets to think before he says or does something and allows subconscious Father's criticism to show through. Then the group starts to affirm what Boy-Father's internal criticism is saying and eats him up. That is why, for the most part, Boy-Fathers only succeed in creating small fiefdoms of control, even though subconscious Father relates to authority as though it were his right to rule.

When Boy-Fathers do succeed in rising to power and use this power for wrong, they can become ruthless and show no compunction. Colonel Kurtz, Marlon Brando's character in the 1979 motion picture *Apocalypse Now,* is a classic example of a Boy-Father who shoots himself in the foot by becoming power-mad.

Orson Wells was a Boy-Father, and his 1941 motion picture, *Citizen Kane,* is another example of how Boy-Fathers can ultimately shoot themselves in the foot after they rise to power. When Kane, the main character, was a child, he loved to ride down the snow-sloped hills on "Rosebud," his wooden sled. Rosebud meant everything to him—a reprieve from a harsh environment and his only way to be a child. Kane's father thought this was foolish and burned the sled, smashing his son's hopes, dreams and innocence. From that point forward, the expectations Kane received from his Father became part of his own subconscious Father mechanism and as his life progressed, he began to outpicture the same destructivity. Kane became the hardened Boychild who has an enormous desire to control others, backed by an incessant subconscious Father drive to dominate.

Like many Boy-Fathers, Kane ultimately shoots himself in the foot. Tyrannical with himself and others, he lives out a miserable life where power and wealth supplant love and intimacy. His days end in Xanadu, a huge estate inspired by Samuel Taylor Coleridge's poem, "In Xanadu, did Kubla Khan a stately pleasure dome decree.*"

As he dies, Kane watches an overturned globe with snowflakes whirling and gasps, "Rosebud." He realizes that all that he has obtained in life means nothing, that all he ever wanted was his Rosebud, and that he has shamed himself to forsake what was dearest to his heart, as his own father trained him.

Unlike Kane, Boy-Fathers who become the Loving Father in action can surmount these difficulties. The Loving Father's impersonality wards off Unloving Father's criticism from within and without. Those who abide within his circle of protection can ultimately find themselves impervious to condemnation. The more Boy-Fathers express this "I and my Father are one" consciousness, the more unstoppable they become in doing what is right for themselves and for others, free from any outside interference.

In most cases, Boy-Fathers genuinely do try to make correct choices and do right by others because of the strong rules inculcated into them as children. They

---

* Samuel Taylor Coleridge, *Poetical Works:* "Kubla Khan." Oxford University Press, 1974

strive to excel in life, even though the process may be slow and wrought with trial and error.

Behind every successful Boy-Father who means well is a loving, supportive and nurturing spouse or parent. Even though Boy-Fathers can be very intense and aggressive, surprisingly, when they come home, take their guns off, hang them up on the door and go into the bedroom, their spouse is usually the boss. If they are not married, their mother usually plays that role.

We can see in late night talk show host, David Letterman, an example of someone who seems to have this pattern and fares extremely well. His relationship with his mother, who often appears on his shows, is very close and touching. She most likely instilled a high level of confidence in him and encouraged him to think twice before doing or saying something. Her nurturing reduced his Boy-Father tendency to shoot himself in the foot, although he regularly does so, turning it into an asset that reveals his unique character and sense of humor.

The best way to cultivate a relationship with a Boy-Father is to provide much-needed Loving Mother and Loved Girlchild support. Behind their rough exterior, Boy-Fathers long for intimacy, even though they do not think they need it. They do not realize how starved they are for affection, because they are so used to depriving themselves of it. In turn, Boy-Fathers must be careful not to bite the hand that feeds them by criticizing or overly dominating those who would care for them.

Then, even though Boy-Fathers may not express their gratitude in an open way, their willingness to stand by their loved ones through thick and thin, without requiring a great deal of attention, will speak for itself.

From Childhood to Adulthood

When a person starts life with subconscious Father, their family tends to be very much into rules, into setting up guidelines for the child to follow. They are expected to take up responsibility and the love they receive is conditional—they must do what they are told. When the children make a mistake, one of the parents may severely discipline them on the letter of the law. As children, Boy-Fathers may end up spending more time with elderly people, like grandparents or elderly neighbors. This provides them with a safe environment where they can let down their guard and be more childlike.

Later in life, Boy-Fathers choose to forget the excessive demands placed upon them as children, along with any pain that resulted from severe discipline. When asked, they will say their childhood was wonderful, because to them, it started when they were fifteen. If you remind them that when they were little, Dad used to hit them hard on the head or Mom always walked them outside without their coat, they will tell you that it was nothing. Even extreme discipline becomes glorified.

At puberty, Boychild starts to challenge his internal criticism. He takes control and decides to forget his childhood injuries. He realizes that if he turns off the volume on his emotions and refuses to give them any power, they will no longer exist, so he completely walls himself off and denies his pain. In doing so, Boy-Fathers can no longer deeply access their feelings, which are sealed over with several layers of concrete but succeed in leading fairly normal, contented lives.

Superconscious and Unconscious Archetypes

Boy-Fathers have double masculine primary archetypes so it is especially important for them to access their feminine superconscious and unconscious archetypes in order to bring balance to their lives. They can have either a superconscious Mother and an unconscious Girlchild or vice-versa. Finding the placement of these two archetypes offers greater insight into their behavior.

Boy-Father with Superconscious Mother and Unconscious Girlchild

Superconscious	Mother
Conscious	**Boychild**
Subconscious	**Father**
Unconscious	Girlchild

Boy-Fathers with superconscious Mother and unconscious Girlchild feel they have a right to be in charge, because they are tough. They are always seeking the all-encompassing, unconditional love of their superconscious Loving Mother and continually try to milk the Mother energy out of whatever situation they are in. Mother also supplies them with the "who, what, where, when and why," which they know makes them successful.

This can make them vulnerable to people who would take advantage of their longing to be mothered. They must be careful not to idolize those who are extremely aloof by pursuing the so-called "pearls of wisdom" that drop from their mouths. They must guard themselves from the smother-mother types who lead them astray by pandering to their self-infatuation, like yes-men who destroy a company by tweaking data to conform to what the boss wants.

Because they have unconscious Girlchild, the last thing these Boy-Fathers want to encounter is Girlchild, whom they judge as whiny, stupid and worthless. When other people behave in a Girlchild way, these Boy-Fathers can become very irritated, because they have completely cut themselves off from this aspect of themselves. Moving against Girlchild, however, does not serve them. They need her finesse and intuition and must learn to honor her feminine presence.

Boy-Father with Superconscious Girlchild and Unconscious Mother

Superconscious	Girlchild
Conscious	**Boychild**
Subconscious	**Father**
Unconscious	Mother

On the other hand, Boy-Fathers with superconscious Girlchild and unconscious Mother pursue Girlchild. They are extremely linear, yet aspire to the spherical, nonlinear side of life. The challenges they face come, because they reject the Mother.

Unconscious Mother indicates they were abandoned in some way and left alone to pull it together. Their massive subconscious criticism of Mother prevents them from fully materializing the Girlchild awareness they seek. If they could, they would take heaven by force and are not above using chemicals, drugs and mechanical devices to get their way. They can be sucked in by illusion and be vulnerable to charlatans or anyone who can produce a certain amount of phenomena. They want divine intimacy without having to learn the lessons of life that Mother brings.

They frantically search for the ghost in the machine but reject every attempt to delineate the "who, what, where, when and why" explanation that "pencil-necked, pointy-headed intellectuals" would exact from them. Instead of looking for miracles to pull them out of difficult entanglements, they must find self-discipline and go through the Loving Mother steps, so they can find a way out on their own.

Family Myths

Boy-Fathers are more influenced by their socialization archetype than people with other patterns. They can appear radically different when their family myths vary.

Boy-Father with a Boychild Family Myth (Most Common)

Boychild	Conscious Boychild
Family	
Myth	Subconscious Father

Boy-Fathers with a Boychild family myth are hardworking and competitive. They can find it difficult to gather a group of supportive individuals to help carry out their ambitions, but they often use money as a substitute for loyalty. They initially come off as shiny, likable people, but their double Boychild energy can eventually put people off. Their Boychild drive is quite aggressive and direct, even though these Boy-Fathers believe they are only "telling it as it is." Coupled with a subconscious masculine energy, it is very hard for them to sustain any level of intimacy. They tend not to get along well with people and often end up alone.

They usually acquire a lot of money from hard work, inheritance or other means and tend to become more and more stingy and eccentric in old age. Like Ebenezer Scrooge, they may end up living out their lives in solitude, which fulfills their hidden Girlchild victim pattern.

Boy-Fathers with a Boychild myth must remember the maxim, "If you live by the sword, you die by the sword." Otherwise, their triple masculine output and their thrust for control, dominance and keeping order can get the best of them. In their push to carry out subconscious Father's will, they become overly aggressive, thinking might makes right, and shoot themselves in the foot. They really need to learn the lesson that you must "do unto others as you would have them do unto you."

Boy-Father with a Mother Family Myth (Common)

Mother	Conscious Boychild
Family	
Myth	Subconscious Father

Boy-Fathers with a Mother family myth are blessed, because they are trained to socialize with dignity and composure through a very feminine and personal presence. Their socialization pattern helps them become very successful in life. Their Mother myth buffers Boychild's mental aggressiveness and makes Father's plans more attractive to others. When Unloving Mother is activated, they become more aloof or distant. This makes it harder for them to carry out their plans, although their adult sophistication still gains respect from others.

Boy-Father with a Girlchild Family Myth (Rare)

Girlchild Family Myth	Conscious Boychild
	Subconscious Father

Boy-Fathers with a Girlchild family myth are under great duress. The grand agendas of subconscious Father, supercharged by the drive of conscious Boychild, run full tilt into the quicksand of their Girlchild family myth. It is like having a superstock race car on a tiny island where the speed limit is five miles per hour, and the journey so short it would be better to walk.

Most of the people who have this pattern are hampered by it. They find it hard to survive and be competent in life. Those who are most besieged may end up in a place of care, be it incarceration or institutionalization. Those who succeed in managing and transcending this archetypal pattern will be seen as those who can "walk on water."

Boy-Father with a Father Family Myth (Extremely Rare)

Father Family Myth	Conscious Boychild
	Subconscious Father

Boy-Fathers are challenged by their double masculine archetypal pattern and subconscious Father criticism. Adding a Father socialization pattern on top of this would be extremely stifling, and the individual would likely react by completely surrendering to the lusts of power and control. To resist misusing the extra power that a Father myth brings would require Herculean strength. Those who succeed would socialize through the Loving Father and consecrate their power to overturn tyranny and uplift humanity, rather than to dominate others.

Boy-Fathers at a Glance

◆ Boy-Fathers have a shiny, magnetic presence.

◆ They are hardworking, rough-and-ready individuals who conquer difficult challenges.

◆ They are great heroes in any crisis and shine in the thick of the fight.

◆ They tend to have a harsh childhood but usually do not remember it.

◆ They can sabotage themselves through self-criticism and by not caring enough about other people's feelings.

◆ Boy-Fathers lean toward orthodoxy and toward hard and fast rules. They can be relentless.

Thirteen

The Analysts

*Problems cannot be solved
by the same level of thinking that created them.*
–Albert Einstein

People who have a dominant conscious Mother and subconscious Boychild (Mother-Boy) pattern rely on the combined strength of conscious wisdom and nurturance with subconscious action and capability. Like Boy-Mothers, Mother-Boys appear complete unto themselves. Their Mother archetype provides the wisdom their Boychild seeks, and Boychild supplies the action principle that archetypal Mother innately lacks.

Mother-Boys seek to find the mystery of life by unfolding wisdom. They have technical understanding, mathematical awareness and are analytical and precise. They often become involved in scientific, analytical or structural endeavors and want to share their findings. They like to teach and can bury others with their facts and empirical logic.

They tend to dominate events by knowing more than anybody else about what is going on. They can also be extremely good salesmen, because they can capture a person's interest through the sheer amount of information they have.

Mother-Boys are essential on any team, because they are effective organizers, will loyally and tirelessly serve to the end and can accomplish great things. They can be counted on to be shock absorbers in any situation—to be moderators in a group, to reduce the potential of a volatile and negative outcome and to keep it together in clutch times. They become the mortar between the bricks and the buffer between the jolts.

Mother-Boys thrive on situations where they can rule from both their adult mind and their visceral Boychild gut instinct. When the going gets tough, when all of the conscious Girlchild types are ready to crawl under the table and all of the conscious Boychild types are getting ready to punch, Mother-Boys can remain adult—poised, calm and collected—and pull through. They have the endurance to carry a project to the end. Even in a long business meeting when everyone is ready to pass out from exhaustion, they keep plugging through the agenda like a Duracell or an Energizer bunny, saying, "Now, item fourteen...."

They do not like being stuck in a back room and usually end up in front-line positions where, ironically, they help others rise to power but do not seek a supreme position of authority for themselves. Even when they have the most competence, they still prefer to let somebody else lead. A lot of Mother-Boys end up either as executive secretaries to the CEOs or as vice-presidents. In a sense, they are always at the wedding as the bridesmaid, never the bride. This means others can access all of their ability, wisdom and strength without worrying about competition.

There are exceptions. George Washington was probably a Mother-Boy. The rough-and-tumble nature of his subconscious Boychild bubbled under all of his mature, well-thought-out actions. He was intellectual enough to partake in British parliamentary procedures but still had the Boychild gumption to take action when he realized his countrymen were being abused and treated as third-class citizens. It took time to elicit a martial response from him, but when his Loving Mother had assembled enough facts, his Boychild moved with assuredness, never looking back.

This was also true of Abraham Lincoln, who probably had the same pattern of behavior. Lincoln's conscious Mother archetype gave him the maturity to be steadfast in the face of adversity, so his subconscious Boychild would keep on keeping on. Nobody thought he would amount to anything. He even went bankrupt several times but never stopped studying to prepare himself for the day he might be called upon for greater service. When he found the right cause, he persevered unto the end, guiding America through the civil war and abolishing slavery.

Since Mother-Boys have learned to handle their emotions in childhood, they expect everybody else to do so. When they come across someone with a dominant child archetype who seems out-of-control emotionally, they think, "Here's somebody who needs to be straightened out," and they relegate that person into the "need-to-be-corrected" bin for an indefinite period of time.

This is especially tricky when Mother-Boys try to correct their boss, often in spite of themselves. Brian once witnessed a situation where Patrick, a Mother-Boy, locked horns with Jennifer, his superior, because he felt compelled to correct her. Patrick said, "Well, the problem with what you're doing is that you're doing it wrong," which didn't go over very well. "What! How dare you tell me I'm doing this in error!" said Jennifer. "I'm the specialist in this field and I know what's right!" Consciously, all Patrick was looking for was acknowledgment of his authority and expertise, but Jennifer interpreted this as a take-over maneuver.

Mother-Boys look for someone they trust to help them see where their Boychild is misbehaving. Then, if their trust is abused, they start rejecting outside feedback and bulldoze their way through life. In the worst-case scenario, they may become rageaholics—mentally aloof and emotionally ruthless—especially if as children, they learned to deal with their emotions by becoming angry.

The best thing for Mother-Boys is to activate their Loving Father archetype and embrace his code of conduct, so subconscious Boychild does not get out of hand. Radio talk show host, Art Bell, successfully demonstrates how to manage Boychild zeal within Loving Father parameters. He is always in contact with aggressive, interrogative Boychild energy coming from his callers or, likely, even from his own subconscious, and yet he has the mental competency and maturity to steer it into channels of constructive use.

Mother-Boys have the innate maturity to nurture healthy relationships but must guard against their subconscious tendency to be one up on others. They need to keep in mind that people sometimes feel small around them, because they are extremely capable and have so much self-confidence. After all, it is difficult to open up to someone who does not seem to need you as much as you need them. It would also benefit Mother-Boys to loosen up in social situations instead of figuring out how to covertly control others.

When Mother-Boys behave in a self-effacing way, which is often the case, and do not appear threatening, other people will embrace the presence of the Loving Mother that emanates from them and welcome them with open arms.

From Childhood to Adulthood

As children, people with subconscious Boychild tend to have rather strict parents and are challenged to gain control of themselves. They are either successfully trained to be "good boys" and "good girls," or they become uncontrollable, difficult and aggressive.

Francis, one of Brian's clients, was a subconscious Boychild child who was a challenge for his parents. His father nicknamed him "little devil" and was ready to send him off to military camp. Then, when Francis started shifting into conscious Mother, he said to his mom, "I'll make you a deal. I'll behave and you do not have to worry any more." "How does the deal go?" she asked. "That's the deal," he said and he never misbehaved again.

Caroline's client, Dennis, on the other hand, was an obedient child. When he moved into his extremely Mother archetype, he started running into problems in groups. Caroline explained to him that because he had, as a child, completely submitted his control to his parents, his pent-up frustration later manifested as subconscious resentment against authority figures, which he had to work through.

The transition of Mother-Boys into their Mother archetype reinforces their need to be in control of themselves and others. In general, though, it is a good experience and brings added competency to subconscious Boychild's action principle.

Superconscious and Unconscious Archetypes

Mother-Boys can either have a superconscious Father and an unconscious Girlchild archetype or vice-versa. Finding the placement of these two archetypes offers greater insight into their behavior.

Mother-Boy with Superconscious Father and Unconscious Girlchild

Superconscious	Father
Conscious	**Mother**
Subconscious	**Boychild**
Unconscious	Girlchild

Mother-Boys with superconscious Father and unconscious Girlchild are usually very successful people. They have no problem fitting in. With superconscious Father, they continuously seek to enforce the law and can go with the letter of the law. Those who cross the line better beware!

Their unconscious Girlchild gives them a tendency to victimize people, without even knowing it. They do not have much respect for Girlchild, especially if she whines about their discipline. When they receive negative feedback, they tend to be aloof to it. For the most part, their lack of consideration for Girlchild feedback is not challenged, because most people only look for results and these types know how to get a job done.

Mother-Boys with Superconscious Girlchild and Unconscious Father

Superconscious	Girlchild
Conscious	**Mother**
Subconscious	**Boychild**
Unconscious	Father

Mother-Boys with superconscious Girlchild and unconscious Father are also very successful in the world and are likely to be teachers of some sort. Superconscious Girlchild gives them a softer touch that complements the maturity and wisdom of their conscious Mother.

Adept at moving through the mazes of life, they unconsciously work their way around Father's standards of obedience. Their Mother-Boy dexterity gets them almost anything they want, and their superconscious Girlchild lets them know how to influence people, which makes them supreme schmoozers at any gathering, business or otherwise. They also appear to be very linear, intellectual and logical, when, in fact, they are really seeking the mysteries of the universe. The challenge is that Boychild wants Girlchild's magic without having to adhere to Father's rules.

These Mother-Boys need to understand that Girlchild cannot be controlled or quantified. They also need to beware of charlatans who would take advantage of their desire to receive feedback from others. Further, they need to stand guard against unconscious Father criticism. They must stop criticizing others for things they do not like in themselves and understand that the success they are looking for will come when this happens. When they learn to replace Unloving Father behavior with the Loving Father's impersonality, the universe will reward them with the mystical creativity they secretly yearn for.

Family Myths

Just as Mother-Boys are influenced by their superconscious and unconscious archetypal pattern, so they are influenced by their socialization archetype.

Mother-Boy with a Boychild Family Myth (Most Common)

Boychild Family Myth	Conscious Mother
	Subconscious Boychild

Mother-Boys with a Boychild family myth may have a lot of suppressed subconscious anger. As children, they often resent having to obey the disciplines set by those who surpass them on the totem pole of family hierarchy. Later in life, they may release this pent-up frustration in social situations by responding aggressively to others, even though they tend to be completely aloof to the fact that they are doing so.

In their early teens, these Mother-Boys learned to dedicate themselves to a purpose in life. Then, as the years pass, they work to the bone to prove their social competence and to bring in the sheaves. Their greatest growth comes when they begin to appreciate the inspiration of their Loved Girlchild, which balances out their intellectual and logical side and softens the subconscious aggressiveness they often release in social situations.

Mother-Boy with a Mother Family Myth (Common)

Mother Family Myth	Conscious Mother
	Subconscious Boychild

As children, Mother-Boys with a Mother family myth really want their family to acknowledge them but do not usually receive the attention they are looking for. They compensate by becoming very competent in their field of work and by working to the bone to prove their worth.

They tend to be confident at the subconscious level but have trouble relating to others in an intimate way. They still harbor resentment towards the aloofness they received in childhood and do not see why others should be emotionally nurtured when they were not. Oftentimes, releasing aggressive emotions is the only intimacy they know and behind their quiet, subdued appearance hides an explosive encounter waiting to happen. If they can learn to overcome this challenge and manage their internal conflict, they will be able to help manage conflict outside of themselves and become the pillars of any community.

Mother-Boy with a Girlchild Family Myth (Rare)

Girlchild	Conscious Mother
Family	
Myth	Subconscious Boychild

Mother-Boys with a Girlchild myth were often raised in chaotic homes where boundaries were not enforced. As children, they figured things out in odd ways. They were often rejected by others, no matter how hard they tried to be accepted. They may have gone right into other people's houses, seeking to escape the chaos of their childhood home, where they were perceived as being a little funny, strange or annoying because of their lack of boundaries.

Later in life, they often suppress their childhood memories. They look for a particular niche where they can shine but are hypersensitive about being rejected. They do well helping others who are downtrodden and who can appreciate the delicate, sensitive interface they have to offer in circumstances that require a total commitment, such as missionary and social work. They are able to handle the high-end chaos that comes with these vocations, because it reminds them, in many ways, of their childhood home environment.

Mother-Boy with a Father Family Myth (Extremely Rare)

Father	Conscious Mother
Family	
Myth	Subconscious Boychild

Mother-Boys who would socialize through a Father myth would appear even more adult in front of a public and would be even more likely to become in charge. With Unloving Father, they would be extremely cool operators—socially impersonal, mentally aloof and emotionally aggressive in a department of intelligence, CIA/NSA-style, that provides an outlet for subconscious Boychild to covertly control others. Those who would choose to socialize through the Loving Father would become capable of organizing an enormous thrust for action with the indefatigability to carry it out. The masculine side of their nature would be amplified, transforming them into great warriors, like Leonidas, the Spartan general who changed the course of Western civilization at the Battle of Thermopylae.

Mother-Boys at a Glance

◆ Mother-Boys are scientific and analytical, and they like to share their findings with others.

◆ They are great organizers and can be shock absorbers in any situation.

◆ They are very adult and expect other people to control their emotions.

◆ They depend on others to give them feedback and can become vulnerable to others' opinions.

◆ They love to teach.

Fourteen

The Nurturers

Be kind, for everyone you meet is fighting a harder battle.
–Plato

People who have dominant conscious Mother and subconscious Girlchild (Mother-Girl) archetypes are the "gentle folk." They know how to nurture others. Consciously they are wise and like to teach, and subconsciously, they are caring. Their Mother energy is warm and personable, and their Girlchild energy is soft, kind and beautiful. They have great sensitivity and are able to mother life in the most delicate ways, but they lack masculine energy, which can be problematic—especially when they are male.

Brian has this pattern of behavior. When he was six years old, he was fighting with another boy through his Boychild family myth pattern, and he was winning the fight, which would have made his dad happy. At a certain point, when his opponent started to cry, Brian wanted to comfort him. He felt terrible. He can remember holding him, and tears came to his eyes. "Don't cry too!" the other boy said, upset by Brian's sensitivity.

Because of the challenges Mother-Girls often experienced in childhood, they can feel another person's pain and understand it from that person's perspective, instead of from an outsider's point of view.

Mahatma Gandhi had this archetypal pattern. He could relate to the oppression of others in a personal way, because he had experienced it within himself through his Girlchild sensitivity. His Mother competency gave him the wisdom strategy to look after the wounds of his own subconscious Girlchild and that of others. When he traveled to South Africa, it dawned on him that people needed more than personal emancipation—they needed cultural emancipation. Thus, as the Mother freeing her own Girlchild, he freed India by fasting and praying British control away, along with any vestiges of brutality within his own nature.

Mother-Girls can also merge, at some level, with the people they are communing with or giving advice to. This can be a very powerful asset. For instance, Deepak Chopra, M.D., seems to have this pattern of behavior. His Girlchild archetype gives him the sensitivity and finesse to tune into a more subtle spiritual understanding. Meanwhile, his Mother archetype gives him the wisdom, the maturity and the strategy to hone in on the needs of the people to whom he is teaching, so he stays very personable while he reaches out to greater and greater numbers.

Mother-Girls can absorb other people's thoughts, feelings and energy like a sponge. They innately understand what other people want and often cave in to the pressure of these spoken or unspoken expectations, which can sometimes be uncomfortable.

When Brian was sixteen, he and his friends hid a huge pile of beer out in a field for a bush party later that evening. At nightfall, all his friends showed up with their girlfriends and nobody could find the beer. Finally, Big Jeff spoke up. "I'm thirsty. You know you can find this," he told Brian. "Remember when we were kids and you knew where all the presents were hidden? Remember at school you were the one who could always find the answers? All you have to do is focus. Close your eyes and remember."

Brian tried to retrace his steps but it was not working. Everybody was getting more thirsty and impatient by the minute.

"That's it," said Big Jeff, in a threatening voice. "Get up and walk off into the bush."

"This will get me out of here," Brian thought, as he started walking and lo and behold, he stumbled upon the beer.

Like most people with developed feminine archetypes, Mother-Girls tend to have a certain amount of psychic ability and can even tap into the elemental essence of inanimate objects. When Brian worked on his family's farm, he would drive a combine—a large, complex harvesting machine—all night long. Eventually, he would become one with the machine. He could feel through the hydraulics, through the sound of the grain being threshed. He could tell when something was not right, long before the gauges set off an alarm. It was almost like part of his body had a special tingling twitch and he could find the itch.

Like Farmer Hoggett in the 1995 motion picture, *Babe*, who tunes into his pig's potential to work as a sheep dog, most Mother-Girls also have an uncanny ability to commune with animals. Brian had an enormous Siberian Husky, Ralph, who never came into the house and neither ate people-food nor dog-food—only his kill. As large and as wild as he was, he would insist on climbing inside Brian's coat like he did when he was a puppy with imploring eyes. "Forget it!" Brian told Ralph over and over again. Still, he would give in enough to pick him up and carry him around, and Ralph was in bliss.

When Mother-Girls function from their loving archetypes, they are like shepherds, tending their flock.

Their intuition becomes a fount of wisdom, understanding and inspiration for others to partake in. Sufi poet, Mevlana Jalaluddin Rumi, was an example of this.

Rumi was already a spiritual leader in his community when his teacher appeared, seemingly from nowhere. Much to the chagrin of his followers, Rumi's feminine, conscious Mother mind became filled with the alpha presence of his teacher and his soul was set free. Then, when Rumi's teacher mysteriously passed on, some say by foul play, Rumi's Girlchild lost her mooring, and Rumi found himself walking around a pole, gloriously praising God. As the dove of his own Girlchild descended upon him and alighted his mind, Rumi was awakened to the depths of wisely nurtured, intimate care that wove a tapestry of absolution in every verse flowing from his mouth.

Like Mother Teresa who devoted her life to the "refuse of life" in the slums of Calcutta, Mother-Girls would give everything they have to someone in need. When Brian was a small boy, he scraped up enough bottle money to get on a bus and go to the fair with his youngest uncle, Jack, who was only a few years older than him.

As they got to the gates, Jack said, "You wait here. I'll see if I can get us in through the horse barn," hoping his connections would let them in for free. Meanwhile, a little man with no legs rode by, putting his tweed hat out to the crowd. All the money in Brian's pocket went into the little tin can the man had nailed to the plank of his skateboard.

Jack came back unsuccessful. When he realized Brian had given away all of his money to the legless man, he tossed his own money into the can with disgust. Then they walked back to the bus station and rode the fifty miles home.

When Mother-Girls cannot set boundaries for themselves, Girlchild feels victimized, and Mother becomes aloof to the fact that they are not keeping anything for themselves. Eventually, they may feel justified in never giving again.

Mother-Girls respond to those who would push them around with passive aggression, be it in a marriage, in a work environment or, like Gandhi, with an entire nation. When they subconsciously experience resentment towards someone, they will consciously ignore or abandon the person. People expect Mother-Girls to really give of themselves, and when they go aloof, the juxtaposition of the two behaviors is very hard for others to accept.

Mother-Girls know how to give intimacy. They know how to recognize what is most wonderful in a person. With them, we can experience the most incredible connection. On the flip side, Mother-Girls can use their psychic sensitivity to manipulate and control others. They can sweep through your subconscious and seduce you by telling you what you want to hear about yourself. They are kings and queens of codependency. They know how to make it so that others become hooked to the level of intimacy they supply.

To avoid giving all of our power away, we must observe whether our desire to be with a Mother-Girl is appropriate and establish parameters through the Loving Father. It is alright to tell them, "I understand that this closeness you want with me is a thing that we all yearn for, but I keep this for my God, my spouse and myself." Then, we can be free of their magnetism.

Likewise, Mother-Girls can establish their own healthy boundaries. The more they engage their Loving Father archetype, the more they can stop giving in to other people's expectations and experience balanced relationships.

From Childhood to Adulthood

Like anyone with subconscious Girlchild, Mother-Girls tend to be vulnerable when they are children and that vulnerability often magnetizes aggression. They learn to protect Girlchild by covering her up.

Their intuition makes it so that they often absorb what other people are thinking or feeling. When they move into their conscious Mother archetype, they retain their feminine sensitivity to other people's thoughts and feelings. This can be overwhelming. To cope, they often bury their childhood pain and deny Girlchild in themselves and in others.

Moving into an adult archetype is nevertheless a wonderful experience for Mother-Girls. They become more competent in groups and feel like they have something of value to offer. Even if at first, they may not notice they are changing, other people will. Their newfound maturity and reserve starts serving them well and makes them extremely competent and savvy with others.

Superconscious and Unconscious Archetypes

Mother-Girls have double-feminine primary archetypes. Their supplementary archetypes are masculine—superconscious Father and unconscious Boychild—or vice-versa. Finding the placement of these two archetypes offers greater insight into their behavior.

Mother-Girl with Superconscious Father and Unconscious Boychild

Superconscious	Father
Conscious	**Mother**
Subconscious	**Girlchild**
Unconscious	Boychild

Mother-Girls with superconscious Father and unconscious Boychild tend to look at God as Father and expect their authority to come from him, along with a certain sternness in the letter of the law.

They can get off track by building powerful personality cults that lead people down the wrong track. They must guard against their unconscious Boychild need to be the center of attention and stop catering to other people's expectations in order to be popular, instead of relying on their own better judgment.

Mother-Girl with Superconscious Boychild and Unconscious Father

Superconscious	Boychild
Conscious	**Mother**
Subconscious	**Girlchild**
Unconscious	Father

Mother-Girls with superconscious Boychild and unconscious Father seek to establish a relationship with a personal God and want to represent him. They often act as though they are divinely inspired and can make others believe that this is so, even though they tend not to believe it when they close the door and face themselves.

With unconscious Father, they often allow other people's expectations and criticism to define them. As a result, they may doubt the value of their Girlchild offering, until they learn to reestablish a strong sense of self-esteem through healthy Loving Father boundaries.

Family Myths

When we run into Mother-Girls, it is very useful to recognize their family myth archetype, because they chameleonize so strongly to what their families expect of them.

Mother-Girl with a Boychild Family Myth (Most Common)

Boychild Family Myth	Conscious Mother
	Subconscious Girlchild

As children, Mother-Girls with a Boychild family myth often attract a lot of positive attention from adults. At the same time, they can be victims of classmates or family members who take advantage of their Girlchild sensitivity. As teenagers, they learn to suppress those hurts and become popular with the in-crowd. Their subconscious Girlchild knows how to mold to what other people want, and they fit right in with little effort.

Impelled by their Boychild family myth, they learn to manipulate others to become the center of attention. They win other people's allegiance by telling them exactly what they want to hear. Instead, they must learn to draw healthy boundaries around themselves and curb their excessive Boychild ambition. Then they will truly earn the respect and the attention they long to receive from others.

Mother-Girl with a Mother Family Myth (Common)

Mother	Conscious Mother
Family	
Myth	Subconscious Girlchild

Mother-Girls with a Mother family myth can be extraordinarily caring or extraordinarily aloof and flip-flop between the two extremes. Adult and poised in social situations, they either come across as nurturing and wise (Loving Mother) or use aloofness to solicit attention from others (Unloving Mother).

Even though they want to love everybody, they find it hard to genuinely give of themselves. When they do not feel safe, they shut down the caring side of themselves and cut people off, especially if their Girlchild was seriously injured in childhood. The more they are sought after, the more aloof they become.

Mother-Girl with a Girlchild Family Myth (Rare)

Girlchild	Conscious Mother
Family	
Myth	Subconscious Girlchild

Once a great warrior was asked, "Why cannot you be caught?" He answered, "The truth is, I'm a fake within a fake within a fake, and I myself have lost my own coordinates, so I cannot be caught."

This is what some Mother-Girls with a Girlchild myth are like. The more they have been trained in a dysfunctional, chaotic way, the more unpredictable they become in social situations. With their triple, nonlinear, feminine energy, they are very hard to pin down. When we run into them, nothing is what it appears to be.

People with this pattern tend to morph with the groups they come into contact with so that they can fit in and belong. They seek to conform, avoiding any confrontation and latching on to a dominant figure. They can serve as very good back-up people, but if they hook up with somebody who is tyrannical, they will not exercise the needed discernment to break free.

Mother-Girl with a Father Family Myth (Extremely Rare)

Father	Conscious Mother
Family	
Myth	Subconscious Girlchild

It would be easy for Mother-Girls with an Unloving Father socialization pattern to rise to a position of power and then ostracize people who reflect back to them their own Unloved Girlchild, turning them into scapegoats. These Mother-Girls might use their psychic abilities to gather information on their victims and then make way for burning crosses and smoking crematoriums.

Mother-Girls who would choose to socialize through the Loving Father, on the other hand, would be able to really nurture the people placed under their care, because they would be impermeable to outside criticism and negative public opinion. The Loving Father would also give them the strength to state a difficult truth or discipline a behavior that is out-of-line without giving up on those who commit a transgression.

Mother-Girls at a Glance

- Mother-Girls like to nurture life and take care of others.

- They lack masculine energy.

- They have great sensitivity and can easily read others.

- They would give everything they have to someone who needs it.

- They can become aloof when they feel offended or taken advantage of.

- They have a wonderful connection with people.

Fifteen

The Creators

The aim of art is to represent
not the outward appearance of things,
but their inward significance.
—Aristotle

People with a dominant conscious Girlchild and subconscious Boychild (Girl-Boy) are wonderful front-line people. They love to interface with the public, and they have a nice soft touch and comfortable presence. Their conscious Girlchild makes them open, available and sensitive to other people's needs.

Girl-Boys are extremely creative and often gravitate towards non-linear, artistic occupations. They tend to be the ones who lay the golden eggs in any organization. As with Boy-Girls, their double-child archetypal charm gives them a powerful stage presence. They can make people believe in them and relate to them on a personal level.

Girlchild at the conscious level is extraordinarily sensitive and caring. She is demure, she has a melodic voice and she would not say "boo" to a goose. Yet behind Little Red Riding Hood hides a big bad wolf—subconscious Boychild aggression.

This makes Girl-Boys unpredictable. Subconsciously, Boychild is always keeping track of things, using Girlchild as his scanner. If somebody gets out of hand,

Boychild's automatic defense pattern comes out to deal with the situation in a rough-and-ready way.

The hidden toughness of Boychild behind Girlchild's carefree, sensitive and sometimes naïve front is often played out in motion pictures by female actresses like Cameron Diaz, Meg Ryan and Lisa Kudrow, among others. People are drawn to their fragile charm and also impressed by their no-nonsense response to challenging situations that can surface when least expected.

The character of Frodo, in *Lord of the Rings*, also plays out this archetypal combination. Humble, innocent, and seemingly reserved, Frodo seems unlikely at first glance to be the best candidate to carry the ring of power that once belonged to the Dark Lord Sauron and that determines the fate of Middle Earth. Even though Frodo is unsure of himself, he is determined to safeguard Middle Earth from the powers of darkness contained in the ring. His inner strength, determination and bravery surface as the epic unfolds. As he faces each challenge put before him, his subconscious Boychild's tenacity always backs up his conscious Girlchild's careful, intuitive strategy and will to do good.

People who have subconscious Boychild do not look like the fighting type and, therefore, take everyone by surprise. Some think they are dealing with "Hello, kitty" but find out they really have a tiger by the tail. Behind their easygoing Girlchild front is an indefatigable Boychild who can outlast everyone.

Ralph, Brian's Siberian husky, was very territorial and decided he was the only animal allowed around the farmhouse. Any other animal was eaten or chased away. Every year, a porcupine would walk across Ralph's turf. It looked so harmless and demure. Ralph would go after the porcupine with his Boychild attitude, as if he were thinking, "That's it, stupid Girlchild deserves a bite for venturing out on my land."

Ralph never figured out why an animal that was so non-aggressive would give him so much pain when he attacked. It only made him angrier and he would bite again. This went on for years and years. Brian would be working in the shop on farm equipment and Ralph would come whining in. He was ashamed that he got the porcupine quills again, but his face was so swollen and infected that he could not stay away. Ralph would put his head on Brian's lap and Brian had to use pliers to pull out the porcupine quills, which gave Ralph even more pain. Ralph never learned his lesson. To the day he died, he thought porcupines should listen to what he thought was right and stay off of his turf.

Likewise, Girl-Boys may look like they are a piece of cake but if you give them a bite, you will suffer long-term ramifications, because they are as tough as nails inside. Girl-Boys usually cannot recognize that they could have any intention to harm, and they are often able to convince others of their harmlessness. Nevertheless, they can become formidable foes when you step on their Girlchild's toes.

Like Maria in *The Sound of Music*, Girl-Boys ever so much want to be the joy, the light and the pink in every room. Even when their aggressive victim pattern is obvious to others, they themselves are usually unaware of just how much aggression they release. It is also difficult for them to take responsibility for their subconscious Boychild's excessive drive for control.

If they are confronted, they use Girlchild as a front. "How can you say I'm over-controlling when I am such an easygoing, accommodating person?" they exclaim. Then they become offended. They do not see that deep inside them lies a Boychild counter-punch to the aggressive treatment they may have received as children.

When Girl-Boys are upset, they can fill a room with the negativity churning from their subconscious and not even notice. Negative energy appears to be innocuous but is far more powerful than it seems. Like the water that seeps through the cracks of boulders, freezes and then shatters the rock in the winter, causing a landslide in the spring, so the crystallized negative Girl-Boy energy can collapse the matrix of an organization and provoke a landslide that few can withstand.

To release their creativity within the confines of a structure, Girl-Boys need direction and guidelines that do not stifle them. Otherwise, all of their creativity will be lost as they balk against what corrals them and activates their victim pattern.

In dealing with Girl-Boys, we need to understand that something difficult transpired in their lives to make them behave the way they do. Once their subconscious Boychild knows we have no intention to harm, he will relax while we talk to Girlchild, who will shower us with her blessings.

Having a conscious Girlchild archetype is not easy. Conscious Girlchild continuously runs into the collective stigma against her delicate, fragrant expression, and magnetizes criticism, abandonment and ruthlessness to herself. This was the case with Princess Diana, who ultimately had to secretly team up with a crew of journalists and resort to making home videos, in order to express to the world the pain, neglect and disregard that she had experienced behind her fairy tale life. Her Girlchild perspicacity and her Boychild courage are also evident in her sharing, ahead of time, that she knew "they" were seeking to kill her.

Girl-Boys long for a sense of connection with others, but first, they must learn to forgive those who have hurt them in the past. This can be tough, especially in the face of those who do not understand their injury and want them to get over it immediately. Girl-Boys must learn to say, "I am no longer the victim, and therefore, my power no longer resides in you." It is their key to personal overcoming. They must also be willing to acknowledge when subconscious Boychild is misbehaving. If they do not, they will appear hypocritical to others, who will detect Boychild's plots under Girlchild's projection of innocence, easygoingness and goodwill.

As Girl-Boys strengthen the inner connection to their Loving Father-Mother archetypes, great healing can take place. It will transform their relationships by setting a solid platform of trust and respect from which they can reach out to others.

First, they must learn to consciously practice the presence of their adult superconscious archetype. Then, they can once again practice wearing the adult archetype they rejected, which is the one that operates in their unconscious. The more they do this, the more empowered they will become and the more their creativity can emerge.

Girl-Boys find no difficulty tuning into their muse—the source of their creative power and divine inspiration. Their intuition is astonishing, and they are usually right on the money. Brian's client, Sally, once gave him a portrait of a child that she drew. When he asked her why she was giving it to him, she told him she thought he might be interested in it. Then she asked him who he thought it was, and he could see the inner child of someone they both knew. Several months went by and Brian began to date the person in the portrait. Today she is his wife, Therese.

Sally exemplifies the extraordinary perception of people who have the Girl-Boy pattern of behavior. When they are loved and accepted, they show us time and time again that they often know more than *they* even know they know.

From Childhood to Adulthood

It is difficult to transit from subconscious Boychild to conscious Girlchild. As Boychild, Girl-Boys are used to being rough-and-ready and having center stage. When they move into Girlchild, they experience a newfound timidity they do not like. Accustomed to their Boychild abilities, they all of a sudden find themselves in a very soft, nebulous and delicate place.

Often, they resent the shift towards Girlchild and overemphasize Boychild to compensate for their newfound vulnerability. If they will tie themselves to a purpose that allows their creativity to flow, welcoming Girlchild will be easier.

Brian was counseling Randy, a teenager who was transiting from Boychild to Girlchild. He was rebelling against his emerging sensitivity, because he thought it made him weak and that other boys could see his vulnerability. Brian reminded Randy that he had just won an acrobatic skiing competition. He said to him, "The final jump that you did, how did you know just where to hit it?"

"I do not know," Randy replied. "I saw something glittering and I knew that if I put my skis there, a little wider than usual, I would get my jump.

Brian asked him, "Do you know that your Girlchild is intuition? She's the one who gives you this knowing."

"What do you mean?"

Following his own intuition, Brian pulled out a deck of cards, picked three cards and put them down in front of Randy. "Okay, now pick one of them and rearrange the others, and my Girlchild is going to find the card you picked," Brian said, secretly hoping his own Girlchild would come through, and she did. Then, he asked Randy to pick the cards he had chosen. At first, Randy was skeptical, but when he picked three out of three right cards, his eyes opened wide. All of a sudden, he realized that having conscious Girlchild was like having a secret agent to help his Boychild win in different competitive events. He embraced his emerging Girlchild self, because he saw how she could give him an edge on the road to success.

Superconscious and Unconscious Archetypes

Girl-Boys have double-child primary archetypes. Like Boy-Girls, it is especially important for them to access the adult qualities of their superconscious and unconscious archetypes. Girl-Boys can either have a superconscious Father and an unconscious Mother archetype, or vice-versa. Finding where these two archetypes are placed offers greater insight into their behavior.

Girl-Boy with Superconscious Father and Unconscious Mother

Superconscious	Father
Conscious	**Girlchild**
Subconscious	**Boychild**
Unconscious	Mother

Girl-Boys with superconscious Father and unconscious Mother have amazing intuition combined with an automatic knowing of how things go. They seek to bring forth spirit in their life through discipline. Because they have a double-child pattern, they may look for someone else to fulfill their need for discipline and can be vulnerable to abuse from those who may play the role of guru for them, especially when they run into someone who embodies Father.

With unconscious Mother, they find it difficult to learn from their peers. They would rather receive teaching directly from their own divinity. Resolution comes to them when they can discern divine authority in the truth that is spoken through another person and can see God in everyone they meet.

Girl-Boy with Superconscious Mother and Unconscious Father

Superconscious	Mother
Conscious	**Girlchild**
Subconscious	**Boychild**
Unconscious	Father

Girl-Boys with superconscious Mother and unconscious Father have an innate ability to deliver the caring of their superconscious Mother through their Girlchild in artistic forms of expression, creating a wonderful rosy ovoid to draw everyone in. The challenge comes from subconscious Boychild, who devises many plans but only has conscious Girlchild to carry them out for him. He tells her, "Now we're going to do this and that," but she's busy finger painting!

Unconscious Father also makes them vulnerable to authority figures, and they tend to draw criticism from those who want to know where their wisdom comes from, just as the Pharisees questioned Jesus, asking, "By what authority do you speak?"

Their best-laid plans may fall apart because of the criticism. Therefore, it is imperative for them to appreciate their value and face the criticism head-on instead of simply hiding in the skirts of superconscious Mother. Superconscious Mother eventually draws them to the place where they recognize they cannot have other people defining them but instead must embrace their own self-discipline and ultimately define themselves.

Family Myths

Just as Girl-Boys are influenced by their superconscious and unconscious archetypal pattern, so they are influenced by their socialization archetype.

Girl-Boy with a Boychild Family Myth (Most Common)

Boychild Family Myth	Conscious Girlchild
	Subconscious Boychild

Girl-Boys with a Boychild family myth are extremely intuitive and creative and are usually drawn in front of an audience by their Boychild myth. This makes them uncomfortable, because conscious Girlchild is intimidated in public, even though subconscious Boychild has a lot of ambition.

In social situations, they tend to hide their Girlchild, descend into their subconscious coping and then generate a Boychild faux pas. Over time, they learn to stop engaging people to protect themselves, which may come across as being aloof. They feign to ignore what is going on, hiding in the deep grass where no one will find them, but eventually their Boychild's need to be the center of attention draws them into the spotlight again.

The key is for them to learn to establish the Loving Father's impersonality, so that they can find protection from within, harness their social drive and bring forth their creativity. Until then, they will feel uneasy in social situations and be awkward with those who interact with them.

Girl-Boy with a Mother Family Myth (Common)

Mother Family Myth	Conscious Girlchild
	Subconscious Boychild

Girl-Boys with a Mother myth are challenged when other people detect that under their apparent adultness, they have a double-child combination. Once their mask has been stripped, they are either rescued or rejected.

They are especially vulnerable to Boychild types who question their authority with an agenda that says, "You only appear to be in charge. I can see your vulnerable Girlchild and I will push her around until you give up, and then I'll be the one in charge." Sanctuary, once again, lies in developing Loving Father boundaries that will protect Girl-Boys from interrogation and reinforce their adult socialization pattern.

Girl-Boy with a Girlchild Family Myth (Rare)

Girlchild Family Myth	Conscious Girlchild
	Subconscious Boychild

Girl-Boys with a Girlchild family myth are very much in touch with others but encounter many challenges. They are incessantly drawn into codependent relationships and therefore, need to establish strong boundaries.

Those who succeed in transcending the limitations of this archetypal assignment can do wonders. O Sensei (Japanese for "great teacher"), who founded the martial art form of Aikido, was most likely a Girl-Boy with a Girlchild myth. He learned to harness the energy of his double Girlchild nature and use it to connect with a higher source of inspiration. This gave him a technique of self-defense known as "moving Zen" that redirects an attacker's energy to overthrow him without harm.

Girl-Boy with a Father Family Myth (Extremely Rare)

Father Family Myth	Conscious Girlchild
	Subconscious Boychild

Someone with a Girl-Boy pattern who socializes through an Unloving Father myth would be eccentric and strange and might create disturbing and macabre art forms. They would exhibit an odd, self-effacing quality, while maintaining a ruthless, emotional hammerlock upon their circle of influence.

Girl-Boys who would choose to socialize through the Loving Father, on the other hand, would connect with their muse under the Loving Father's shield of protection. Uplifted by his presence, they would achieve new heights of artistic perfection that exalt life.

Girl-Boys at a Glance

◆ Girl-Boys are extremely creative, artistic and intuitive.

◆ They want to be the joy, the pink, the comfort in every room.

◆ They appear to be easygoing and accommodating but can become aggressive in a pinch.

◆ They need direction and guidelines that do not stifle them.

◆ They often receive criticism and abandonment from those who do not appreciate their gifts.

Sixteen

The Inspirers

Let the beauty of what you love be what you do.
—Rumi

People who have a dominant, conscious Girlchild and a subconscious Mother (Girl-Mother) pattern live to inspire others. They supercharge unconditional love with Girlchild care and finesse. Conscious Girlchild spends her time thinking about how she can help people, and subconscious Mother provides her with the "who, what, where, when and why" to do so.

Subconsciously, they know how to give others the nurturing, teaching, guiding and unconditional love they want without expecting anything in return. People generally feel safe and relaxed in their presence, which gives them a lot of power and control. They often serve in lines of work like nursing or counseling. They also gravitate to the world of dance where many are ballerinas, living for a beauty that transcends the beauty they have seen.

Girl-Mothers can appear childlike. When they are not under pressure, they often speak in a musical and high-pitched tone, like the Girl-Boys. At the same time, they have a lot of emotional maturity. All of a sudden, at the drop of a hat, they may say something extremely wise and mature that catches us off guard. They can also endure through the most difficult circumstances.

Actress Sally Fields portrays this archetypal pattern of behavior in much of her work. Under the bubbly, Girlchild enthusiasm parodied in her famous statement, "You love me, you love me, you really love me," lies the no-nonsense strength of the Loving Mother. This strength was especially apparent in her role in *Not Without My Daughter,* a 1991 motion picture about the true story of a woman who went to all ends to leave Iran with her daughter and succeeded against all odds.

Girl-Mothers are healers. They have an incredible ability to bring forth deep resources within themselves, to mother life, to contact divinity and to pull down extraordinary creativity. Girlchild and Mother are both chalices for spirit, and Girl-Mothers bring Holy Spirit magic in a way that is tangible to the world. The Italian singer, Andrea Boccelli, seems to do this well. His work and his entire being emanate Girlchild love, goodwill, inspiration and innocence that have moved audiences around the world. Yet under his childlike beauty, we can perceive the wisdom and nurturance of Loving Mother, helping him successfully move through life in spite of his blindness.

Girl-Mothers like to know how the body works and often get involved in other people's health. They are drawn to natural health regimens. Others sometimes think they go overboard and label them as "health freaks," but they are just trying to be fastidious and earnest about taking good care of their bodies and want to convince everyone around them to do the same.

No matter what their field of work, Girl-Mothers show tremendous creativity. Sometimes, their gifts are hard to measure, because they are subtle and non-linear. They may appear to be empirical, but their knowledge comes from their intuition. Einstein most likely had a Girl-Mother pattern. He intuitively received the theory of relativity as a flash of inspiration, and then he reverse engineered the answer to make it seem as though it came from writing long equations. He knew that he needed to submit a logical sequence in order for his theory to be received by the scientific community.

Girl-Mothers also have psychic abilities. They read people as a natural defense mechanism, checking for any malintent. Even so, they sometimes still lack discernment and let others take advantage of their generosity. Then, when they feel mistreated, they become aloof and are unable to resolve the situation.

If somebody says, "I'm sorry about what happened the other night," they'll say: "What other night? What do you mean? Nothing's wrong, sniff."

"I know I did something."

"Oh, no, that didn't bother me at all—sniff."

Then, there is silence for days, and the offensive person may from that point forward be erased from Girl-Mothers' lives. The juxtaposition of these two energies is hard for others to deal with—basking in a beautiful pink ovoid of unconditional love one moment and being abandoned the next.

People long to be mothered and Girl-Mothers so much want to respond to that need. Like Mother-Girls, Girl-Mothers must be careful not to create codependent relationships with others. They must also be wary of "love at first sight," because they can fall in love or have others fall in love with them passionately, quickly and sometimes superficially. Many times, though, this love does prove to be true, so discernment is key.

When Girl-Mothers hold an inflated opinion about themselves, they will seek to tie themselves to people who will confirm that opinion and prop them up.

Then, their motive for caring becomes selfish—to generate idolatry from others through seeming altruism. They must guard against facilitating the worst in others in order to receive approval, and they must also guard against doing good deeds only to boost their self-image.

When Girl-Mothers learn to become impersonal through their Loving Father archetype, they no longer have to depend on others for the positive feedback they seek. Then, they can truly care for life with no strings attached, because their self-esteem is internally generated.

Being Girl-Mother can be especially challenging for men. Caroline's client, Sean, struggled with this pattern. Sean had a daughter who was going through her teenage years, and he knew that if he did not get on top of his over-accommodating Girl-Mother behavior with her, neither she nor her boyfriend would respect his authority. He had to work especially hard to compensate for his double feminine side by anchoring his Loving Father archetype, bringing online the masculine energy needed to deal with the situation.

Developing the Loving Father is crucial for Girl-Mothers to build healthy relationships. Otherwise, even if they know how to love and open up, they will feel trapped when they are caught off guard by their own sense of victimization, triggered in the most unexpected ways. With the Loving Father, they can protect their conscious Girlchild and bring in the masculine energy needed to balance their double-feminine sensitivity. Then, they can truly stop giving their power away to those who offend them, forgive them and be free.

From Childhood to Adulthood

As children, Girl-Mothers function from their subconscious Mother archetype. They often have adult responsibilities and a certain autonomy. Then, when they reach puberty, they transit into a child feminine archetype, which is difficult, because it is a diminutive role. After feeling competent and grown up, they become vulnerable and childlike, and can no longer use their adult energy up front.

"What's happened to me?" they wonder. It is like Bob Dylan's song lyrics, "I was so much older then, I'm younger than that now.*" Generally, they cope with the change by becoming aloof.

Usually, Girl-Mothers either escape the family orbit and find someone to latch onto, or stay to serve the family until everyone around them has passed on. Those who leave need to be cautious not to become drawn to people who would abuse of their willingness to serve. As long as Girl-Mothers exercise discrimination in their relationships, they can bring great healing and inspiration to others and draw out the best in them.

Superconscious and Unconscious Archetypes

Girl-Mothers have double-feminine primary archetypes. Their supplementary archetypes are masculine—superconscious Father and unconscious Boychild—or vice-versa. Finding the placement of these two archetypes offers greater insight into their behavior.

---

* 1964; Bob Dylan, "My Back Pages"

Girl-Mother with Superconscious Father and Unconscious Boychild

Superconscious	Father
Conscious	**Girlchild**
Subconscious	**Mother**
Unconscious	Boychild

Like all Girl-Mothers, Girl-Mothers with superconscious Father and unconscious Boychild aspire to God as Father and can automatically download blueprints. They are very much in touch with divinity but can be seen as "flakes" by others. When Jesus said that the meek shall inherit the earth, he could have been describing this archetypal combination.

They often attract Boychild aggression from others, who lust after their inspiration, ferret out their vulnerability and would have them be their slave. They cope by being emotionally aloof to this Boychild aggression, but it would benefit them more to pull down the boundaries of superconscious Father, who will not allow conscious Girlchild to be trampled by anyone.

Girl-Mother with Superconscious Boychild and Unconscious Father

Superconscious	Boychild
Conscious	**Girlchild**
Subconscious	**Mother**
Unconscious	Father

Girl-Mothers with superconscious Boychild and unconscious Father pursue the dynamic side of God, who can take down the walls of Jericho. They are attracted to people who impersonate that quality of Boychild and can become over-involved with them.

Therefore, they must exercise discrimination when choosing which star they would tie themselves to and not become fanatical. Otherwise, conscious Girlchild will morph to fit a group's expectations and may behave in insensitive, even ruthless ways, which do not complement her gentle nature.

Unconscious Father makes these Girl-Mothers vulnerable to criticism. As children, they were expected to be adult early on, and every time they fell short of the mark, unconscious Father criticized them. This early challenge has made them reticent to do things that might draw fire from unconscious Father and the people their subconscious projects this power onto.

Instead, they must learn to practice the presence of the Loving Father, so they will not be so vulnerable to other people's opinions. As they become more impervious to outside criticism, they can truly deliver their gifts of healing to the world.

Family Myths

Just as Girl-Mothers are influenced by their superconscious and unconscious archetypal pattern, so they are influenced by their socialization archetype.

Girl-Mother with a Boychild Family Myth (Most Common)

Boychild	Conscious Girlchild
Family	
Myth	Subconscious Mother

Girl-Mothers with a Boychild family myth yearn for recognition and are attracted to public situations, where other people focus on them. Sometimes they can become quite zealous about sharing their gifts and converting other people to their way of thinking, taking their enthusiasm on the road like singer, Neil Diamond, describes in his song, "Brother Love's Traveling Salvation Show."

Their Boychild myth can also generate aggressive energies from others, which is hard on conscious Girlchild, who is uneasy about having to be in public in the first place. When their Girlchild feels vulnerable and seeks to hide out, people with this pattern fall back onto their subconscious Mother archetype and respond with aloofness.

Girl-Mother with Mother Family Myth (Common)

Mother Family Myth	Conscious Girlchild
	Subconscious Mother

Girl-Mothers with a Mother myth have a social and a subconscious buffer of Mother energy to protect their conscious Girlchild archetype, and they use social and emotional aloofness to protect her. They appear to be antisocial loners, but they secretly want others to engage them. What they really want is a way to release their Girlchild creativity in an environment where no aggressive energies will be exchanged. Otherwise, their Girlchild can safely emerge only when they are alone.

Girl-Mother with a Girlchild Family Myth (Rare)

Girlchild Family Myth	Conscious Girlchild
	Subconscious Mother

Growing up, Girl-Mothers with a Girlchild family myth learned to use their subconscious Mother to hold the balance for the chaotic situations triggered by their family myth. This innate understanding of their Mother archetype, combined with their conscious awareness of Girlchild, gives them the ability to better handle the challenges brought on by a Girlchild family myth. They fare better than most people at being unconventional.

Girl-Mother with a Father Family Myth (Extremely Rare)

Father	Conscious Girlchild
Family	
Myth	Subconscious Mother

Girl-Mothers with an Unloving Father socialization myth could get out of hand in their drive to care for others. They might rule those who fall under their dominion with a vice-like grip, "loving them to death" for obscure psychological, social or spiritual reasons, like we saw in Jonestown.

In contrast, Girl-Mothers who embrace a Loving Father socialization pattern would draw healthy boundaries to protect and seal themselves and others. This would allow them to bring forth that creative, inspired and harmonic style of music, science or health regimen that is theirs to accomplish with unbound potential.

Girl-Mothers at a Glance

◆ Girl-Mothers love to inspire and heal others.

◆ They can appear childlike and think in non-linear ways.

◆ They live for beauty and have tremendous creativity.

◆ They use their psychic abilities as a defense mechanism.

◆ When injured, they may succumb to an aloof pattern of denial.

◆ This combination is especially challenging for men.

Seventeen

The Overcomers

Our greatest glory is not in never falling,
but in rising every time we fall.
—Confucius

People with a dominant conscious Girlchild and subconscious Father (Girl-Father) pattern are rare and complex individuals who tend to be attracted towards many different lines of work. Conscious Girlchild seeks to help others with caring, sensitivity and finesse, but Father downstairs only wants to dominate the world with his rules and guidelines. "Now we must incorporate the ten commandments," he tells her, or "We've got to get rid of all the bad guys on a global scale right now."

Subconscious Father has stocked up tanks in the basement but depends on conscious Girlchild to carry out his plans. "Yes, I agree with you one hundred percent," Girlchild tells him. "Let's all hug." It is like trying to hammer a nail with a piece of linguini.

Subconscious Father needs everything straightened out immediately. People with this combination have a very strong perfectionist mechanism and high expectation of themselves. Years ago, Brian traveled through Greece with Craig, who was in the U.S. armed forces and turned out to be quite a historian. As they got up into the mountains of Sparta, Craig said, "Here are the drowning pools."

"What are those?" Brian asked.

"Well," he explained, "back in Sparta they used to throw the babies into the ice cold pools, and only the ones who could swim to the edge got to live. They used a long wooden pole to prod the baby girls further out into the middle of the pool and the boys closer to shore." Having to satisfy subconscious Father's extreme expectations is a similar duress for Girlchild.

When people come across a Girl-Father type, they first encounter the softness of Girlchild and everything is warm, fuzzy and inviting. Then, once they get to know them and subconscious Father comes out, zing—they find that under the velvet glove is a fist of iron. Subconscious Father comes out in a pinch, when everyone least expects him, and he is very intense. It is like biting into something soft, chewy and sweet—and chipping your tooth.

The Father energy Girl-Fathers release tends to offend others, because most people are uncomfortable with it. When Girl-Fathers succeed in outpicturing the Loving Father, however, their competencies are very impressive. They can bring out the Loving Father more easily than any other archetypal pattern, because they have had so much practice with it. This is their gift.

News reporter, Barbara Walters, is a good example of someone who has succeeded in bringing forth her Loving Father archetype. Regardless of the story she covers or the people she interviews, she demonstrates objectivity, fair play and an authoritative presence. She knows how to bring a discussion back to center in an impersonal and professional way. The care and finesse of the Loved Girlchild, combined with the no-nonsense assurance of the Loving Father gives her a wide range of competency and depth of feeling that can bring out what is most relevant in every story. The mastery she has with her archetypes contributes greatly to her success.

Girl-Fathers bring us an unparalleled opportunity to acclimate ourselves to Father energy, even though initially, we may find it disturbing. Consider, for instance, TV court Judge Judy. The Father energy she has internalized comes out in everything she says. She does not mince words. She says it like it is. She does not spare those who step outside of the law, and ignorance is never an excuse. Yet her Girlchild caring shines through her gruffness, making it more palatable. Even though she is stern, you know that she takes everyone's best interests to heart and goads them to a higher place.

When we come across Girl-Fathers, we must recognize that they only want what is best. Instead of reacting negatively when they become too pushy, we need to be kind, generous and patient with them, and remember that having subconscious Father is not easy.

Subconscious Father, to conscious Girlchild, is like a grim reaper lurking in the bushes waiting to strike. His criticism seeks to tear down whatever she is doing. It also tends to magnetize criticism from others, which then provides Girl-Fathers with an opportunity to be injured by somebody else. Even if the outside criticism matches what subconscious Father has been saying all along, he does not take it well. He will not tolerate that others abuse Girlchild with the same criticism he regularly dishes out. Then, when conscious Girlchild says, "Let's give that person another chance," subconscious Father will most likely refuse.

Girl-Fathers either keep ahead of their criticism pattern or get eaten up by it. They must put aside their jadedness, and their lust to criticize and to be criticized. They must earnestly practice the presence of the Loving Father to become more adult, impersonal and dexterous with their handling of life and its problems. They must be willing to say, "Every person who I believe seeks to harm me has been sent to expose my worst enemy—my own internal criticism pattern, to show me once and for all that I must stop letting it define me. When someone points out things that I am already criticizing myself about, I will stop taking offense. I will become impersonal and constructively deal with my failings. I will see this one as a messenger who comes to teach me, and I will bless them for the lesson they bring to me."

Even if this seems utopian or unrealistic, it is important to try. Remember there is true power in the word TRY. Like the grandmother who tells us: "If at first you don't succeed, try, TRY again," those who persevere always come out ahead.

As Girl-Fathers learn to harness Father's energy to protect Girlchild instead of to criticize her, they gain mastery. They build a solid platform of self-esteem from where they can reach out to others. So long as their Unloving Father shoots out criticism and cruel remarks, ignoring conscious Girlchild's protests, Girl-Fathers will not experience the sense of connection they yearn for.

In the Book of Job, we read the story of a man who experienced much travail early in life and was blessed beyond measure in his late years. Girl-Fathers have a Jobian combination. They are great overcomers who tend to be rewarded as the years go by and who mellow out in time. When they finally resolve the dichotomy between their subconscious Father and conscious Girlchild, and conquer their internal criticism pattern, they become unstoppable. They can share their victory with others and be instruments of healing and conversion.

Along the way, they can profess, "As I help others, so am I helped. As I heal others, I heal myself. As I confront the criticism that burdens somebody else, I learn to dismantle my own. As I help others find their way out of their Hades, I find a way out of my own."

Years ago, Caroline heard a story about workers in a field. One worker was given a large stone to carry for years and years; another was not. After many humiliating years of not measuring up, the worker with the stone had learned to keep up and even excel. Then, one day, he was relieved of his stone and the worker who had never carried a stone could no longer keep up with the other worker's newfound freedom, endurance and strength.

The story is an archetypal story about Girl-Fathers. Like the worker in the field, if Girl-Fathers will only forgive those who have placed burdens upon them and keep on keeping on, they will find that in time, their stones will be removed. Then, they will walk as the greatest among us and inspire us to follow in their steps.

From Childhood to Adulthood

Girl-Fathers usually had difficult childhoods that forced them to function through a Father archetype from square one. They may have been expected to look after themselves and to make their way, following a strict code of conduct. They may have been required to do everything perfectly the first time and received heavy criticism otherwise.

Sandy was hit by a car when she was little. She was in her driveway when a neighbor's car turned in from the boulevard, pinned her up against her house and broke her legs. The driver happened to be the neighbor's older daughter who had taken the car without her parents' permission. She got out of the car, thinking: "My parents are going to kill me," and was running around in circles.

Sandy's parents' immediate reaction was, "What's this noise out here? How did you get the neighbor's car to pin you up against the wall? And what are we going to tell the neighbors?" They did not even back the car up. Their message to Sandy was, "You're supposed to look after yourself and look at what you've done. You interrupted our television program and now we have to come out and look after you." Begrudgingly, they took her to the hospital.

Even in less extreme situations, having subconscious Father indicates that, as a child, Girl-Fathers were forced to compensate for a lack of adult structure around them. They may put on a Father archetype, because, in an unconscious way, their parents did not provide an adequate blueprint for them to function through, forcing them to rely on their internal Loving Father archetype from square one.

Teenage years can be very challenging for Girl-Fathers. Moving from an adult and masculine archetype to a child and feminine archetype is testing. After practicing the most demanding archetype for years, they start to exercise a seemingly weak and sensitive archetype at the conscious level. Their adolescence is similar to the transition from Boychild to Girlchild, only many times more difficult.

Caroline has a Girl-Father pattern of behavior. She was the eldest child and was forced to look after her entire family. Her mother had abdicated her role, and Caroline ruled the roost, bringing order to chaos—to the extent that a child could actually do so. When she started moving into puberty, her younger sister decided she wanted to be boss. Because Caroline was becoming more Girlchild all the time, her sister took advantage of this newfound vulnerability and toppled her leadership. Her other siblings also capitalized on the situation, but her parents still expected Caroline to hold the family together.

Most Girl-Fathers have a hard time getting over their childhood pain, and they tend to be disconnected from their family, because being with the family brings up difficult memories. Those who succeed in bringing forth the Loving Father's circle of protection can learn to genuinely get over their childhood injuries or sense of lack. Then, they can use the Loved Girlchild's forgiveness to heal any rifts that were created in the past.

Superconscious and Unconscious Archetypes

Girl-Fathers either have superconscious Mother and unconscious Boychild archetypes, or vice-versa. Learning where these two archetypes are placed offers greater insight into their behavior.

Girl-Father with Superconscious Mother and Unconscious Boychild

Superconscious	Mother
Conscious	**Girlchild**
Subconscious	**Father**
Unconscious	Boychild

People with a superconscious Mother and an unconscious Boychild pattern are always looking for the unconditional love of Mother to come and correct all the problems in their life. When this does not happen, they are left with a hypercritical Unloving Father in the subconscious continuously telling them how inept and worthless their Girlchild is. As a result, they can spiral into a deep funk if life is not continually pouring unconditional love on them. When they conquer this victim pattern, they can achieve great accomplishments, because they are much stronger for it. As long as they focus on overcoming rather than on being done to, and on forgiving rather than on criticizing, the Loving Mother will grace them with nurturance and wisdom.

Their unconscious Boychild attracts enormous criticism from those who are envious of their abilities. When they retaliate with Unloving Father's subconscious criticism, everybody loses. Instead, they need to bring out the Loving Father's impersonality to draw healthy boundaries that protect themselves and others.

Girl-Father with Superconscious Boychild and Unconscious Mother

Superconscious	Boychild
Conscious	**Girlchild**
Subconscious	**Father**
Unconscious	Mother

Girl-Fathers with superconscious Boychild and unconscious Mother aspire to Boychild and want a dramatic conqueror to save their Girlchild. They look for perfection in themselves and in others and find it difficult to receive information from their peers, unless their peers embody some measure of perfection. Those who fulfill their stringent expectations can literally become Godlike to them.

Girl-Fathers with superconscious Boychild must guard against their need to idolize seeming perfection or to raise others to a superhuman position, lest they be greatly disappointed. They must keep in the forefront of their minds the statement of the real Loved Boychild and learn to abide by it: "I of mine own self can do nothing. It is the Father in me which doeth the works."[*]

Family Myths

Like Girl-Boys and Girl-Mothers, Girl-Fathers tend to morph to what their family myth expects of them, and they strongly play out their socialization archetype. This can make Girl-Fathers appear quite different one from another.

Girl-Father with a Boychild Family Myth (Most Common)

Boychild	Conscious Girlchild
Family	
Myth	Subconscious Father

Girl-Fathers with a Boychild family myth are very sociable and are drawn into public encounters through their Boychild myth. Girlchild finds out just what and who she has to be to meet the situation and usually defers to Father and Boychild. At first glance, other people do not detect her presence, because the person seems to be such serious business. Then, if they step on her toes by mistake, Father and Boychild storm down with full force. In a situation where Girlchild is valued—in an art show, for example—she will come out of hiding and demonstrate extraordinary competency.

---

[*] Paraphrase of John 8:28-29

Girl-Father with a Mother Family Myth (Common)

Mother	Conscious Girlchild
Family	
Myth	Subconscious Father

Girl-Fathers with a Mother family myth are more sophisticated and relate with an adult demeanor. They cover their Girlchild and come off as being Father and Mother, which can serve them well in public. When they are not pushed into a dominant public role, they prefer to be left alone.

Girl-Father with a Girlchild Family Myth (Rare)

Girlchild	Conscious Girlchild
Family	
Myth	Subconscious Father

Girl-Fathers with a Girlchild family myth are very much curtailed by their Girlchild family myth, which reinforces subconscious Father's harshness toward Girlchild. Because they are socially and intellectually porous and have an incredible push for power in the subconscious, they can end up, in severe cases, in institutions where they claim to be Jesus or Napoleon. Those who master their subconscious Father drive and honor Girlchild's gifts, however, can become pioneers in self-transcendence. They embody the maxim, "From my great weakness comes my great strength."

Girl-Father with a Father Family Myth (Extremely Rare)

Father	Conscious Girlchild
Family	
Myth	Subconscious Father

Girl-Fathers who socialize through Unloving Father would seek to externalize their internal self-flagellating tendency upon other Girlchild types under a Kevorkian-like system of care. They might also be found running mental institutions in a pre-Reagan era fashion, ruling the mentally infirm with the same harshness they experienced from their family.

In contrast, Girl-Fathers who would socialize through the Loving Father would be authentic instruments of healing and spiritual reality that is unbiased, impersonal and transcends all religious dogma.

Girl-Fathers at a Glance

- ◆ Girl-Fathers have a rare and complex pattern. The split between conscious and subconscious archetypes is most extreme for them.

- ◆ They have a strong perfectionist mechanism and often have severe self-criticism. They can come off as very intense.

- ◆ They appear to be soft and gentle and surprise people with the harshness of subconscious Unloving Father.

- ◆ They can manifest their Father archetype at the conscious level more easily than anyone.

- ◆ They usually have severe childhood experiences to work through.

- ◆ They are great overcomers.

PART FOUR

A

RELATIONSHIP

GUIDE

Once we recognize our pattern of behavior and study the other seven, we discover a new foundation for building meaningful relationships. We must never use our awareness of the inner family archetypes to put negative labels on people or to manipulate them. Instead, we must strive to consciously develop all four loving archetypes, so that we can respond to people and situations in the most appropriate and compassionate way, at any given time.

Part Four is a guide for relating authentically to others. It builds on the information presented in the previous sections. It gives an overview of how the eight patterns relate to each other, highlighting major opportunities and challenges in each situation.

In every relationship, success ultimately comes to those who, no matter what archetypal pattern they inherited, are willing to be adult, to adopt Loving Father boundaries and to provide Loving Mother nurturing and guidance. When the Loving Father and the Loving Mother govern a relationship, the Loved Boychild's will to accomplish and the Loved Girlchild's creativity is unleashed. Then, both people can contribute their skills and abilities in an interdependent way. They can feel safe to open up to each other and to be honest about their strengths and weaknesses. They are able to supply the difference, especially when they have mastered an archetypal principle with which the other person is still struggling.

The relationship guide that follows will be most useful for those who recognize their pattern of behavior and the pattern of the people with whom they are involved. Please remember that the more someone learns to express their four loving archetypes, the more integrated these archetypes become. Through this refining process, the variance between each archetype becomes subtle, blending into a seamless whole. When this happens, a person becomes less confined to their original archetypal makeup and it may be harder for others to define which combination they are relating to.

To assist you if your pattern or somebody else's pattern is unclear to you, our inner family consultants can guide you, so you can fully benefit from the information presented in this section.[*]

---

[*]For more information, please visit www.innerfamilyarchetypes.com or call 1-877-WHYWEDO.

Boy-Mother Meets Boy-Mother

Boy-Mothers are movers and shakers. When two of them get together, they can have a great exchange of ideas. Then competition may set in, because they like to keep track of the score of who gets more attention. If there is just not enough oxygen in the room for both of them, they may either become emotionally aloof and wander away from each other, or start a fight.

Boy-Mothers need to avoid creating a Boychild competition with each other and pull up their ability to be adult. They need to be flexible enough to say, "Competition is not going to do us any good. If I can be adult and absorb what I'm hearing from this person, I might actually learn something I didn't know before."

Chances are that if they receive each other graciously, they will enjoy a synergistic exchange of new ideas. Otherwise, the best thing for them to do is to listen to the other person, thank that person for their message and move on.

Boy-Mother Meets Boy-Girl

If a Boy-Mother and a Boy-Girl come together, they can get along well because they have similar Boychild energy and aspirations. This is an especially good combination for advertising, sales and marketing because the two can draw upon their combined Boychild stamina, Mother wisdom and Girlchild creativity.

At the conscious level, both people agree to get things done. At the subconscious level, they relate to each other through their feminine archetypes. If one must lead the other, it is better for Boy-Mothers to have the leadership role, because it is easier for Boy-Girls to acquiesce to subconscious Mother's authority than for Boy-Mothers to follow a double-child type.

For a healthy relationship, Boy-Mothers must remember that even if Boy-Girls acquiesce to their leadership, they are not to be put down for being double-child. Boy-Mothers must avoid exacting too much logic from Boy-Girls, especially when subconscious Girlchild does something unpredictable and nonlinear. They must also refrain from tiring of Boy-Girls' Girlchild and responding with subconscious aloofness. Otherwise, they will trip off Girlchild's sense of victimization, abandonment and retaliation.

For a relationship to endure, Boy-Mothers need to refrain from putting down Boy-Girls' spontaneous childlike energy and Boy-Girls need to become impersonal to any perceived injury.

Boy-Mother Meets Boy-Father

Boy-Mothers and Boy-Fathers can get along well, because they know the other person has the same steely determination as their own. Consciously, they create a mutual admiration society and engage in exciting Boychild plans and maneuvers. Emotionally, however, they may not be in touch with what is going on, and Boy-Fathers usually push Boy-Mothers to go aloof. "Let's be adult but no hugging," they say.

Boy-Fathers want to be in charge and Boy-Mothers are used to being in charge. When this poses a problem, Boy-Mothers may try to aloof Boy-Fathers—unsuccessfully, because Boy-Fathers have such a tough underbelly. "So what?" may say the Boy-Father. "You don't care about me? Big deal."

If a Boychild competition ensues between the two, Boy-Mothers may start feeling inferior to Boy-Fathers who, one way or another, subconsciously hook into Boy-Mothers' internal criticism and start reflecting it back. Meanwhile, Boy-Mothers have no recourse, because aloofness does not work.

For a productive relationship, Boy-Mothers will have to acquiesce to being second in command and put up with a certain amount of criticism from Boy-Fathers, even if it is unspoken. If Boy-Mothers will refrain from running Boy-Fathers' failings up the flagpole, Boy-Fathers will lead the team very well. By providing the Loving Mother's "who, what, when, where and why" coordinate points, Boy-Mothers can also compensate for Boy-Fathers' "shoot yourself in the foot" mechanism. Then, the relationship between the two will become indomitable, combining the strengths of subconscious Father and Mother, with the can-do spirit of conscious Boychild.

Boy-Mother Meets Mother-Boy

Boy-Mothers make the world go round and Mother-Boys keep it going. The two have reciprocating patterns and a wonderful synergism together, as Mother-Boys' conscious Mother nurtures Boy-Mothers' conscious Boychild, and Boy-Mothers' subconscious Mother nurtures Mother-Boys' subconscious Boychild. Both people seek to explore the secrets of matter in a complementary way. Mother-Boys can provide the blueprint of what needs to happen, and Boy-Mothers can show Mother-Boys how to make it happen.

Initially, Boy-Mothers may look upon Mother-Boy's adult conscious archetype in a utilitarian way. "This person can serve me well," they observe. "They behave in an adult fashion and can help me accomplish my objectives, so long as they do not become aloof." Meanwhile, Mother-Boys want to believe in what Boy-Mothers are selling to them, because their subconscious Boychild archetype is emotionally idealistic.

It is important for Mother-Boys to stay grounded. If their subconscious Boychild tells them, "Go with this person, because the ideal they are selling will bear fruit," conscious Mother must pull in the reins and say: "Here's somebody who has conscious Boychild. I feel excited around them and we have a fulfilling conversation, but I must not give them control over my life because I have the adult archetype in this situation." When Boy-Mothers' conscious Boychild enthusiam is held in check by Mother-Boys' conscious Mother balance, the relationship between the two can become very productive.

Boy-Mother Meets Mother-Girl

When Boy-Mother meets Mother-Girl, the two generally have a good rapport. Boy-Mothers' conscious Boychild wants to know how to get things done, and Mother-Girls' conscious Mother provides him with the "who, what, where, when and why" to make it happen.

This can be a very complementary relationship with a wonderful conscious combination of wisdom and action, and a subconscious combination of wisdom, creativity, caring and finesse.

Generally, Boy-Mothers cannot resist being in charge and Mother-Girls will acquiesce to that leadership. If Boy-Mothers start taking advantage of Mother-Girls' willingness to serve their cause, their pushiness will fulfill Mother-Girls' subconscious Unloved Girlchild victim pattern, which is not a good thing. If instead, Mother-Girls can help Boy-Mothers act with finesse, Mother-Girls will find fulfillment. Boy-Mothers will recognize that Mother-Girls' touch of care leads to greater success, and they will extend Mother-Girls the success they deserve.

Boy-Mother Meets Girl-Boy

At its best, a relationship between Boy-Mothers and Girl-Boys combines Boy-Mothers' left-brain wisdom and action with Girl-Boys' right-brain creativity.

When the two get together, Girl-Boys may give their control over to Boy-Mothers. In extreme cases, Girl-Boys may become so indentured to Boy-Mothers' ideals that they may feel like they are living someone else's life.

Most of the time, however, Boy-Mothers do not find much in Girl-Boys to catch their interest, because Girl-Boys readily agree with them and do not challenge their authority. Boy-Mothers may even give Girl-Boys a good pinch at the emotional level to provoke a more lively response. Then, when Girl-Boys' subconscious Boychild hisses, Boy-Mothers may deny any wrongdoing. At that point, Girl-Boys would feel both victimized and superior, and abandon the relationship.

The two must be on the lookout for their conscious and subconscious Boychildren competing for Boy-Mothers' subconscious Mother attention. If Girl-Boys' subconscious Boychild gets ignored by Boy-Mothers' subconscious Mother, he might send the person an interrogative energy, which would make them feel even more edgy and activate their aloofness even more.

To avoid this problem, Boy-Mothers can proactively respond to Girl-Boys' emotional need for nurturance, instead of keeping it all for themselves. Then, the relationship will be mutually fulfilling, especially if Boy-Mothers will take the time to appreciate the spherical gifts, the creative intuition and the brilliant ideas that Girl-Boys selflessly bring to the table, which Boy-Mothers may later claim as their own.

Boy-Mother Meets Girl-Mother

Girl-Mothers want to save everybody and mother them along the way. When they run into Boy-Mothers, Boy-Mothers will want to sell them what they have and Girl-Mothers will usually let them have their way. Even though Boy-Mothers will likely take advantage of the opportunity, they will likely secretly judge Girl-Mothers as being off base and a little too easy.

To be respected, Girl-Mothers must recognize that Boy-Mothers expect practical and tangible results from them. They have to relate to Boy-Mothers in a way that shows they are competent, while subconscious Mother holds the balance. One way to do this is to simply ask Boy-Mothers for their opinion. Boy-Mothers will jump at the opportunity to instruct and converse with Girl-Mothers as equals. Girl-Mothers will feel great even if they do not understand half of what Boy-Mothers are talking about.

The key is for both people to exercise some flexibility, recognize each other's gifts and stop putting each other down. Then, their relationship will thrive.

Boy-Mother Meets Girl-Father

Boy-Mothers and Girl-Fathers were both trained in childhood to look after themselves. They fall back on their subconscious adult strength and rise to the occasion in any crisis. They also have conscious child creativity, interest and purity, and can follow the same star. Girl-Fathers are very disciplined, which pleases Boy-Mothers, who are also attracted to their Girlchild energy.

Things can heat up if Boy-Mothers' subconscious Mother becomes emotionally aloof to Girl-Fathers' conscious Girlchild, who picks it up in a heartbeat. Were that aloofness to persist and Boy-Mothers' Boychild to become aggressive, the problem would escalate. Then, Girl-Fathers' subconscious Father would most likely criticize Boy-Mothers' conscious Boychild, who would retaliate by bullying Girl-Fathers' conscious Girlchild.

To avoid this, both people must exercise the adult qualities they have in their subconscious and create clear guidelines for conscious Boychild and Girlchild to follow. Then, they can have a balanced and powerful relationship that draws on the strengths of all their combined four loving archetypes. Centered on a higher purpose—an ideal to shoot for or something of value to pursue—they can be very productive together.

Boy-Girl Meets Boy-Girl

Boy-Girls really like other Boy-Girls, until they get into competition with each other. They may both agree that the world is a nasty place and that people are out to get them. Even though they want to champion a cause or an underdog in trouble, they tend to disagree on how to do it.

One conscious Boychild may vie for control over the other person. Then, when that person's subconscious Girlchild takes offense, the daggers come out.

Once a Boy-Girl's trust has been breeched, it is hard to retrieve it. Each person looks to the other for reparations, not realizing that the other person also feels let down. Unless the two become adult about the situation, their aggressive victim pattern may get out of hand. Their will to harm and counter-harm each other may even reach a level where law enforcement has to intervene.

When two Boy-Girls can place the cause they are serving above their personal ambition or if they have a boss who makes sure they do not get too personal with each other, they can learn to forsake their competition and work well together. Harmonious, they can move mountains with their creativity, their drive and their desire to convert others to their cause.

Boy-Girl Meets Boy-Father

Boy-Girls and Boy-Fathers usually like each other and get along. They want to conquer the world with a mutual Boychild agenda, but they can become impatient, irritated and even aggressive when they get blocked.

If, for instance, Boy-Girls' subconscious Girlchild does something that backfires and Boy-Fathers' conscious Boychild gets upset, he will let subconscious Father's criticism move in on her.

Once Boy-Girls were no longer useful to fulfill an agenda, Boy-Fathers might choose to discard them. This would be very hard on Boy-Girls' Girlchild, and conscious Boychild would seek to avenge subconscious Girlchild through some aggressive counter-maneuver. In this case, Boy-Fathers might not even acknowledge the aggression, because in their mind, the recalcitrant Boy-Girl is already out of their life. Still, when a Boy-Girl's vengeance is ignited, Boy-Fathers would have to pay whether or not they want to admit it.

For a relationship between a Boy-Girl and a Boy-Father to be successful, the two must exhibit Loving Mother nurturing toward one another. In so doing, Boy-Father will value Girlchild and withhold his criticism, and Boy-Girl will feel emotionally affirmed by Boy-Father. Then, the two can accomplish their objectives.

Boy-Girl Meets Mother-Boy

Boy-Girls and Mother-Boys attract and repel each other at the same time. Most of the time, Mother-Boys profess they do not want control and let Boy-Girls call the shots. This arrangement seems like a win-win. Subconsciously, however, Mother-Boys' Boychild does not want to be led by somebody else, and he may kick Boy-Girls' Girlchild in the shins. Consciously, Mother-Boys may not perceive or own up to any subconscious domineering or aggressive behavior. They may minimize a subconscious Girlchild injury, setting off Boy-Girls' conscious Boychild to confront the problem head on.

Once a competition is on, Mother-Boys' subconscious Boychild will wait for Boy-Girls' conscious Boychild to make a mistake, so he can point it out with conscious adult superiority. Then, if conscious Mother responds with aloofness, the offended Boy-Girls may not hold back on how far they will go, and may create an ongoing feud.

The only way for this relationship to work is if Boy-Girls stop underestimating Mother-Boys' competitive edge. Boy-Girls must remember that someone with subconscious Boychild has a lot more experience at being Boychild than they have, because that experience started in infancy. They must also stop turning into aggressive victims.

Meanwhile, Mother-Boys must stop putting Boy-Girls down as childish, with searing superiority. If they will draw upon their Loving Mother archetype, she will help both people work out their wants and diffuse any competitive energy. Then, Boy-Girls can be in charge in a rational, logical and sensible way, and the two can accomplish wonders together.

Boy-Girl Meets Mother-Girl

When Boy-Girls and Mother-Girls come together, Mother-Girls' conscious Mother nurtures Boy-Girls' conscious Boychild, and Boy-Girls' conscious Boychild motivates Mother-Girls to get things done.

Both share subconscious Girlchild sensitivity, which is bonding, but they can also fall into the same emotional victim pattern. Boy-Girls may feel victimized by Mother-Girls' intellectual aloofness, and Mother-Girls may feel victimized by Boy-Girls' aggressive impulses. Childishness from Boy-Girls can also activate Mother-Girls' negative judgment and subsequent aloofness. Then, even if Mother-Girls continue to appease Boy-Girls, they may no longer respect them. This frustrates Boy-Girls' conscious Boychild, who wants a "well done" from Mother-Girls' conscious Mother, and she quickly tires of his demands.

Mother-Girls need to realize that even though they convince themselves and others that they are good judges of character, they actually have a bias. When the person they are dealing with reminds them of someone they are fond of, they more willingly give that person special consideration. Otherwise, they can allocate someone to no-man's land, especially if the person reminds them of someone who affronted them in childhood, which is often the case with Boy-Girls.

Boy-Girls, meanwhile, must stop letting others define them. If they will exercise the power of their four loving archetypes and learn to build their self-esteem from within, they will establish a platform of maturity and wholeness from where to reach out to others. Then, Mother-Girls will not feel so put-upon by Boy-Girls's Boychild expectations, and will treat them with fondness.

Boy-Girl Meets Girl-Boy

When Boy-Girls and Girl-Boys come together, the creative potential is enormous, as is, unfortunately, the potential for victimization, aggression and counter-aggression. In this relationship, Boy-Girls' conscious Boychild wants to be in charge. Girl-Boys may overtly agree, but their subconscious Boychild will start a covert competition. Then, resentment is likely to build between each person's conscious and subconscious Girlchild.

William and Peter were brothers and worked together for many years. They married Jean and Mary, who were best friends in school. When their parents passed on, Peter got the home farm and William got the other farm, just across the fence.

One day, William did not go to the home farm to fix something but fixed it at his place instead. Old Peter thought that was treacherous, because the home farm had all the tools and equipment. It was where things had always been fixed. Then, without telling Peter, William went out and bought a metal lathe. The two brothers had each inherited a Krupps Steelwork lathe from their father, but William had decided to buy a new-fangled American model that came from Pittsburgh.

Peter asked him, "How did you fix that furrow wheel, William, without having to come home and use the equipment?"

"Well, I welded it and ground it down."

"Oh, you did? You've got a welder over there, do you?"

"Yeah, it is just a small one."

A little while later, Peter showed up at William's farm, threw the shed door open and saw William

253

cutting a bar of steel on his new Pittsburgh lathe. He went berserk. His reaction was that of a man finding his wife with a lover.

"What's this thing that we have here?" he fumed.

"Well, it is a lathe. Otherwise, I have to drive all the way over to *your* place."

"*Your* place? That's our home!"

Next thing you know, a barbed wire fence went up between the two farms and the brothers no longer spoke to each other, throwing ignoring glances at each other when they worked parallel fields.

Fast-forward 26 years.

Brian was having something fixed at Peter's place. They went in for some of his famous coffee when the phone rang and Peter's wife, Jean, picked it up. Finally she hung up, looked at them and said, "Well, I cannot believe it. Peter, do you know what just happened? William's youngest son had the gall to call me Auntie Jean when I have never even seen him face to face!"

"What?" said Peter, taken aback.

"Oh, William's dead!" she announced. "And they had the nerve to phone up and call me Auntie Jean and ask us if we'd want to go to the funeral. We never talked to them in 25 years, and what makes them think that we're going to go to the funeral now?"

"What's going on?" said Peter, incredulous. He looked like somebody threw a pail of water on a cat.

They finished their coffee rather solemnly and went back out to the machine shop to finish fixing Brian's equipment. Brian told him, "You know, I'm going to the funeral and I'll be passing right by. I could just pop by and pick you up from the shop. We could sit in the back and no one would know the difference, not even Jean."

Peter's eyes glowed with a sense of resolution and heartfelt sorrow. Then, his face turned dark and he bowed his head and said, "No, I cannot do it. Jean would never understand."

In that moment, Brian realized he was being taught a great lesson. He reached out and took the gigantic, callous-toughened hand of this big, old man. With his head bowed, Peter clenched back, hiccupped two sobs and said, "I'm so sorry."

The truth was that the wives, who were best friends when they came out of school, had adopted the feud. Jean and Mary had a Boy-Girl, Girl-Boy relationship and were so affronted with each other that the brothers had become hostage to *their* vendetta.

If Boy-Girls and Girl-Boys will not forgive each other, they may lock horns for the rest of their lives. If they will stay centered and be reasonable with each other, they will find that they can greatly enjoy each other's lively, effervescent energy.

Boy-Girl Meets Girl-Mother

Boy-Girls and Girl-Mothers can be a highly creative and dynamic team. Boy-Girls' can-do spirit complements Girl-Mothers' inherent wisdom, and both people agree that Girlchild needs looking after.

Initially, Boy-Girls may resist Girl-Mothers' authority, because conscious Girlchild seems disorganized. This frustration simply reflects the ambiguity conscious Boychild feels about his own subconscious Girlchild. Her qualities of caring and finesse do not register to him as sensible or useful. Like the tortoise and the hare, Boychild strategizes that to come out ahead, he must blaze through things, and Girlchild going the extra mile seems like a waste of time.

Boy-Girls' conscious Boychild may want to make sure Girl-Mothers' conscious Girlchild is contained. Girl-Mothers seem to go along with this, but do not to change anything. When Boychild gets dramatic, they do not get swept up emotionally. They always trust their subconscious assuredness over outer Boychild control, which registers to them as puerile and risky.

If Girl-Mothers' conscious Girlchild gets hurt by Boy-Girls' conscious Boychild, subconscious Mother may become aloof and Boychild may become more aggressive. At that point, Girl-Mothers would likely wall themselves off and the two people would disconnect.

To make their relationship work, Girl-Mothers need to empower Boy-Girls to make real decisions, giving them the benefit of the doubt. Boy-Girls must recognize Girl-Mothers' strengths, even if they lie outside of Boychild's area of competency. Then, both people will be able to contribute to the relationship and to the world in creative and caring ways that combine Mother's wisdom and Boychild's action.

Boy-Girl Meets Girl-Father

Boy-Girls and Girl-Fathers can have a good relationship when Boy-Girls' Boychild champions Girl-Fathers' Girlchild, and when Boy-Girls' Girlchild feels protected by Girl-Fathers' Loving Father.

Initially, Boy-Girls may seek to dominate Girl-Fathers and Girl-Fathers will hang back. Then, if Boy-Girls make a mistake, Girl-Fathers' subconscious Father may start to criticize Boy-Girls' subconscious Girlchild, as if it were his own. Boy-Girls' Boychild may launch back, thinking Girl-Fathers' conscious Girlchild is an easy target, and if Father comes out with intensity, he is caught off guard. Boy-Girls would then drop into subconscious Girlchild and flee the scene, or, feel cornered and attack Girl-Father's Girlchild until Girl-Father backs off.

The key for this relationship to succeed is for Girl-Fathers to consciously develop their Loving Father archetype and protect Girlchild instead of criticizing her in themselves and in other people. Boy-Girls, meanwhile, must learn to deal with problems in a more adult way. Then, they will be able to get along with people who operate from a strong adult archetype. They will even learn to model Girl-Fathers' innate adultness, while Girl-Fathers benefit from Boy-Girls' buoyant energy, which brings joy into their lives.

Boy-Father Meets Boy-Father

Boy-Fathers tend to see their job as controlling and directing circumstances. They want to embody the letter of the law, which they believe implicitly gives them the right to rule others.

When two Boy-Fathers come into contact, they admire each other and do not find much to correct in the other person. The problem is that, eventually, they have to figure out which one of the two is going to be boss. Like Western motion picture gun fighters, they may try to eliminate each other by saying, "This town ain't big enough for the both of us. One of us is going to have to go—head first or feet first."

Boy-Fathers can learn to unite through discipline. By following a professional code of conduct, or a boss to who both report, they can iron out their differences. Then, uniting their strengths, they become an indomitable team. Moving toward the same goal with their storng masculine energy, they can part the Red Sea.

Boy-Father Meets Mother-Boy

Boy-Fathers and Mother-Boys work very well together, especially in a business environment. Mother's wisdom complements Boychild's action at the conscious level, and the two share an "I and my Father are one" unity down in the subconscious, as they figure out what agenda they want carried out.

Problems only arise if Boy-Fathers' conscious Boychild wants to be in charge and gets in competition with Mother-Boys' subconscious Boychild. Then, Mother-Boys may walk away or covertly sabotage Boy-Fathers' plans. When Boy-Fathers finally caught up to what was going on and moved to get rid of Mother-Boys, Mother-Boys would care less. To avoid this, the two must stay adult in their interactions and refrain from trying to outdo each other.

Aligned with an unloving agenda, the potential damage of this relationship is enormous, like the Mafioso Boy-Father boss and his "brains of the outfit" Mother-Boy. The opposite is equally true. If both people can work together for a noble cause, they can successfully challenge tremendous odds and become champion-knights.

Boy-Father Meets Mother-Girl

A relationship between Boy-Fathers and Mother-Girls usually fares well. Action and wisdom meet at the conscious level. At the subconscious level, Father wants order, organization and statesmanship, and Girlchild agrees. She wants somebody to be in charge. She likes authority and wants to follow someone who will protect her.

Problems arise if conscious Boychild becomes possessive of the other person. "This is *my* Mother-Girl," he might say. "I do not want to share her with anybody else." He might start to get jealous of anything that takes Mother-Girls' attention away from him, be it another person or the television set.

Boy-Fathers' frustration might push them to criticize Mother-Girls, who would most likely respond with aloofness, while yet secretly hoping for Boy-Fathers repentence. Boy-Fathers lack of sensitivity would impair them from reading through the aloofness. "That's it!" they might say. "I banish you from my world." Then, the relationship would be over.

Boy-Fathers and Mother-Girls must strive to avoid this. They must remember that if their relationship is loving, they will be very fulfilled. Through their union, Boychild has found his Mother and Girlchild has found her Father.

Boy-Father Meets Girl-Boy

Boy-Fathers and Girl-Boys can have an excellent relationship. Conscious Boychild tends to look at conscious Girlchild as somebody he needs to champion, and subconscious Father looks at subconscious Boychild as somebody he can work with to carry out his "let's control the world" agenda. Together, they have a nice synergy. Boy-Fathers want to be in charge, and Girl-Boys readily submit, becoming someone that Boy-Fathers really trust.

A relationship between the two can also be like fire and water. For starters, Girl-Boys may want to ease their way into projects, while Boy-Fathers want to jump in with both feet. Girl-Boys may also seek to correct Boy-Fathers' lack of finesse, and be met with resistance.

"You've got to be careful about saying bald jokes around Uncle Albert, because that offends him," Girl-Boy, for example, chides Boy-Father. Boy-Father then disagrees. "What are you talking about?" he says. "It is no big deal."

If the two do not work on their relationship, Boy-Fathers' Boychild will eventually stop rescuing Girl-Boys' Girlchild, and their Unloving Father will start criticizing her as incompetent. Conscious Girlchild is so sensitive that even if Boy-Fathers' criticism is subconscious, she will pick up on it. Then, the more stressed out she gets about pleasing, the more mistakes she will make, which incidentally fulfills her subconscious Boychild need to retaliate. Were Boy-Fathers to confront Girl-Boys, Girl-Boys would apologize, saying they had no intention of wrongdoing, and likely convince Boy-Fathers that this is so. Still, they would keep making mistakes to covertly punish Boy-Fathers for having criticized them.

Were they to go in for counseling together, Boy-Fathers might be told: "You're projecting all the criticism that you lay upon yourself on Girlchild so she can wear it for you, because you think she's more inept than you are. Stop making her carry your load." Then Girl-Boys' subconscious aggression patterns would have to be confronted. "Stop purposely leaving the spaghetti on the doorknob and saying you didn't mean to," they might be told.

Most often, the therapy would stop there, because Girl-Boys generally do not want to admit that they are purposely doing anything wrong. Meanwhile, Boy-Fathers would capitalize on the situation and hoist Girl-Boys' misdoings up the flagpole for everyone to see. Were the conflict to escalate this far, Boy-Fathers would have a tiger by the tail. Girl-Boys' subconscious Boychild would likely become out-of-control, working full-time to drive them crazy. Ultimately, Boy-Fathers would lose the game, because they lack intuition to detect subconscious Boychild's ploys.

A relationship with Girl-Boys is one of the best lessons Boy-Fathers could ever have. It teaches them that even though some people seem easygoing, they must resist taking advantage of them. Boy-Fathers also offer an important learning experience for Girl-Boys by challenging their covert subconscious Boychild manipulation. Once Girl-Boys become aware of their subconscious Boychild aggression and what it can provoke in others, they can make the effort to change and become that much better for it.

Boy-Father Meets Girl-Mother

When Boy-Fathers meet Girl-Mothers, there is a nice team up of energy. Boy-Fathers like Girl-Mothers, and Girl-Mothers feel safe around Boy-Fathers, knowing that Boy-Fathers will look after them well. The two have double-child creative energy at the conscious level, and Father's discipline and Mother's wisdom downstairs in the subconscious.

Like the relationship between Boy-Fathers and Mother-Girls, this relationship may also get difficult if Boy-Fathers become too possessive of Girl-Mothers. Then, Unloving Father may kick in and start to criticize Girlchild into staying put. If she feels victimized and confined, she would drop into her subconscious Mother aloofness.

At this point Boy-Fathers' Unloving Father might tell conscious Boychild to take Girl-Mothers by force, and become cold, aggressive, even violent. Most of the time, Girl-Mothers would stay because their Unloved Girlchild believes she deserves to be punished, but they would deprive Boy-Fathers of authentic nurturing and care.

For the relationship to work, Boy-Fathers must acknowledge that Girl-Mothers can offer them much needed feminine energy and support. They must recognize that if they truly want Girl-Mothers' loyalty, they have to be flexible and stop restraining them under the guise of looking out for them. Then, Girl-Mothers' gratitude will fully compensate Boy-Fathers for their good will.

Boy-Father Meets Girl-Father

Boy-Fathers and Girl-Fathers generally get along well, especially in a social or business context. They labor together to carry out subconscious Father's agendas. Boy-Fathers usually decide that their conscious Boychild makes them boss and Girl-Fathers agree to submit.

The relationship will start to heat up if Boy-Fathers criticize Girl-Fathers' conscious Girlchild way of doing things. Then, Girl-Fathers may take them by surprise with a "Get in line, buddy, because nobody's heaping it on me more than myself." The two may get into a criticism-fest until Boy-Fathers realize that Girl-Fathers' Girlchild needs to be rescued and stop the criticism. Again, girl-Fathers may take them by surprise because instead of expressing gratitude, they may refuse to give up their self-criticism. Then, the more Boy-Fathers would become invested in saving Girl-Fathers' Girlchild and fail, the more their own subconscious Father would dump criticism on them.

The only way out of this negative scenario is for both people to take a step back and summon their loving adult archetypes. To stabilize their relationship, they need to recognize that the problems that they have with one another actually stem back to childhood injuries inflicted by a critical parent, and stop projecting that parent onto the other person. If they will set their minds to this, their relationship will suicceed, for all challenges have their equivalent reward.

Mother-Boy Meets Mother-Boy

When two Mother-Boys meet, they may feel awkward because of their adult reserve. Consciously, they tend to be very polite with each other and get along well. Subconsciously, their two Boychildren may be throwing darts at each other down in the basement. Their covert subconscious competition is hard for them to define, and conscious Mother does not want to own it. If one Mother-Boy attempts to resolve the situation by apologizing, the other person might deny any problem. Then a crouching tiger, hidden dragon battle would carry on subconsciously beneath polite conscious interactions.

The best thing to stop sabotaging this relationship's potential is for both people to stay adult and find humor in the situation. If Mother-Boys would admit their subconscious drive to be superior and in charge—at least to themselves—and surrender it, they could engage their Loving Father. They could heed the Loving Father's direction that says, "Be your brother's keeper. Forgive him for his need to be superior, even as you forgive yourself for yours. Remember that your worth is not defined by your capacity to control but rather by your capacity to love."

With this honest effort, Mother-Boys will function from a place of true maturity. They will be able to pool their many talents and abilities together and excel.

Mother-Boy Meets Mother-Girl

Mother-Boys and Mother-Girls get along well and usually relate from conscious Mother to conscious Mother. They have a similar viewpoint on life. They believe it is important for people to behave in an adult way, and they tend to avoid volatile situations. They can also be counted on to keep it together when circumstances become trying.

In a relationship, Mother-Boys want to be in charge and Mother-Girls tend to agree. Subconscious Boychild wants to either champion subconscious Girlchild or bully her, and she responds accordingly as his nurturer or as his victim.

If the relationship sours, it is usually because Mother-Girls' subconscious Girlchild becomes hypersensitive to Mother-Boys' conscious aloofness or subconscious aggression. When Mother-Girls' conscious Mother realizes that subconscious Girlchild has been offended, they tend to stop supplying Mother-Boys with the feedback they seek—which drives Mother-Boys into a more aggressive pursuit. Eventually, there may be a complete communication breakdown as both people feel justified in their negativity toward each other.

If, instead, both people avoid letting their subconscious injuries take over and stay adult, they can earnestly serve each other's needs. Mother-Boys can especially help Mother-Girls succeed in a practical, business sense, and Mother-Girls can supply Mother-Boys with trustworthy feedback and friendship.

Mother-Boy Meets Girl-Boy

Mother-Boys and Girl-Boys get along very well. Emotionally, their Boychildren have the same objectives. The only difference is that Mother-Boys count on their wisdom and logic to carry them through, and Girl-Boys count on their intuitive download. Even though Mother-Boys tend to appreciate conscious Girlchild's intuition and creativity, they do not trust it completely. They may end up selectively using Girl-Boys' ideas instead of wholeheartedly embracing them.

If the relationship goes bad, it is usually because Girl-Boys' conscious Girlchild is hypersensitive about Mother-Boys' judgement of her thinking process. Then, her subconscious Boychild can get aggressive. The minute that occurs, Mother-Boys may react with aloofness, and Girl-Boys may further engage Unloved Boychild's destructive intent.

To strengthen the relationship, Mother-Boys need to honor Girlchild in themselves and in others, and Girl-Boys need to forsake their Unloved Girlchild's need to be injured. Then, the two can bypass this confrontation and truly learn to appreciate each other's differences.

Mother-Boy Meets Girl-Mother

In a relationship between Mother-Boys and Girl-Mothers, Girl-Mothers' conscious Girlchild meshes well with Mother-Boys' conscious Mother energy, and Mother-Boys' subconscious Boychild can draw upon Girl-Mothers' subconscious Mother for guidance.

Problems come up if Mother-Boys become consciously aloof and take Girl-Mothers' service for granted. If Girl-Mothers sense this aloofness, it sets off their own subconscious aloofness. Then, Mother-Boys' subconscious Boychild may feel abandoned, and he may retaliate emotionally in an aggressive way.

To avoid locking up the relationship, both people need to to stick to their conscious or subconscious Loving Mother maturity, and to a Loving Father code of conduct. Then, they can ride out these waves and have a mutually satisfying relationship. Girl-Mothers will supply Mother-Boys with the healing they need, and Mother-Boys will supply Girl-Mothers with the worldly competence they lack.

Mother-Boy Meets Girl-Father

Mother-Boys and Girl-Fathers generally get along well. They have similar energy patterns—conscious feminine up top and subconscious masculine downstairs. Mother-Boys immediately assume they should lead, but do not really want to. They pretend to be in charge, and Girl-Fathers go along with them, when, in fact, Girl-Fathers covertly run things.

Problems may arise if Mother-Boys' conscious Mother becomes aloof to Girl-Fathers' conscious Girlchild and allows subconscious Boychild to get aggressive with her. Because their Boychild aggression is subconscious, Mother-Boys can turn off Girl-Fathers without even knowing it. They may not even realize that they have lost an opportunity to have an authentic relationship with someone who can teach them how to engage the Loving Father, which is what Mother-Boys secretly yearn for.

So long as the two relate through their conscious feminine energy, they can avoid these problems. Girl-Fathers will help Mother-Boys self-transcend, and Mother-Boys will provide Girl-Fathers with utilitarian benefits, like a paycheck.

When Girl-Fathers, who are used to managing Father energy in the subconscious, also allow their Loving Father to emerge, their relationship with Mother-Boys will further accelerate. Then, the two will benefit from having all four archetypes readily available. Together, they will be able to draw upon Father's protection, Mother's wisdom, Girlchild's creativity and Boychild's action.

Mother-Girl Meets Mother-Girl

When two Mother-Girls get together, they consciously attempt to mother people, and subconsciously care about not hurting other people's feelings. They affirm each other's viewpoint, which is often the same as their own. They are like twins, and often think or say the same thing at the same time. Even though being able to do this is interesting and flattering at the beginning, it can get old. Then Mother-Girls will look for someone with a different archetypal pattern to give them more variance.

The relationship will only be difficult if one person decides to ignore the other, even accidentally, and the other person feels abandoned. Once one Mother-Girl's subconscious Girlchild picks up on the other Mother-Girl's aloofness, their conscious Mother may also become aloof. Next thing you know, both people would stop communicating, all the while denying that there is any problem between them.

In spite of this possibility, Mother-Girls rarely disagree with each other and get along quite well.

Mother-Girl Meets Girl–Boy

Mother-Girls and Girl-Boys have two conscious feminine archetypes, which gives their relationship a nice, smooth-sailing surface. Both people consciously want to nurture and care for life, and Girl-Boys' subconscious Boychild is completely dedicated to this end. The relationship only tends to be complicated under the surface, where Girl-Boys' subconscious Boychild wants to rules Mother-Girls' Girlchild, even though consciously, Mother-Girls think they should be in charge.

Challenges may also arise if Girl-Boys' conscious Girlchild picks up aloofness from Mother-Girls and feels abandoned or ignored. This would make their subconscious Boychild aggressively pursue Mother-Girls' nurturing, and Mother-Girls might feel oppressed. They might shut down with more aloofness, expecting Girl-Boys to take control of themselves, and Girl-Boys might respond that much more aggressively.

For a relationship to thrive, Mother-Girls have to deal with the tides of Girl-Boys' emotions. They must not take the "You're my best friend one day, you're my worst enemy the next" hyperbole too seriously. Instead, they must provide adult constancy and forsake feeling superior to a double-child type. On their end, Girl-Boys must stop aggressively pursuing Mother-Girls, and embrace them as caring teachers who will forgive much.

Then, the two can enjoy a mutually beneficial relationship. Girl-Boys will provide the intuition and creativity that Mother-Girls can use to flush out their own picture of reality, and Mother-Girls will provide Girl-Boys with loving adult comfort and assuredness.

Mother-Girl Meets Girl-Mother

When Mother-Girls meet Girl-Mothers, they get along well with each other. For the most part, Girl-Mothers feel understood by Mother-Girls and instinctively know they are not going to get hurt.

If the relationship deteriorates, it is usually because Mother-Girls' conscious sense of superiority sees Girl-Mothers' conscious Girlchild as a child who needs correction. This can set off Girl-Mothers' subconscious aloofness, injuring Mother-Girls' subconscious Girlchild. Then both people can lock up in an aloof victim pattern, even though there is rarely, if ever, an overt aggressive exchange.

Most of the time, however, the relationship is very pleasant. Mother-Girls simply need to remember that Girl-Mothers have been practicing an adult archetype since birth and honor that subconscious adultness. They also need to understand that conscious Girlchild may have been wounded in the past, which sometimes causes one to behave irrationally. If Mother-Girls are willing to simply hold the balance for the childlike quality of Girl-Mothers, the two will benefit greatly from each other's nurturing, caring presence.

Mother-Girl Meets Girl-Father

Mother-Girls and Girl-Fathers get along well, with their conscious feminine energy that seeks to nurture and care for life. Girlchild also serves as a buffer between Mother-Girls' conscious Mother and Girl-Fathers' subconscious Father, so they do not attack each other, even if conscious Mother becomes aloof.

Mother-Girls' subconscious Girlchild may at times feel intimidated by Girl-Fathers' subconscious Father, especially if Girl-Fathers criticize their own Girlchild. To avoid being treated the same way, they might decide to hide out behind conscious Mother's aloofness.

The minute this would happen, Girl-Fathers would feel criticized internally and abandoned externally. Subconscious Father might retaliate by taking a few shots at Mother-Girls' subconscious Girlchild, which would only amp up their aloof response. Further offended by Mother-Girls' aloofness, Girl-Fathers might outright criticize them and lock up the relationship.

For things to work out, Mother-Girls must avoid withholding nurturance from Girl-Fathers. Girl-Fathers must also recognize that Mother-Girls have an aversion to Unloving Father's subconscious criticism. If they want a successful relationship with Mother-Girls, they must remember that you cannot truly love others if you do not love yourself first. When they determine to respect and honor their most vulnerable self, Mother-Girls will feel safe in their presence. Then, Girl-Fathers' subconscious Father will find in Mother-Girls the competent and trustworthy partner he was seeking to carry out his plans.

Girl-Boy Meets Girl-Boy

Girl-Boys get along well with each other. They both want to save those who are more vulnerable than they are. As long as they can find a cause to unite them, their subconscious Boychild will carry out the mission.

Problems only tend to arise if the leadership is not clearly delineated between the two, and subconscious Boychild starts to wonder, "Who's in charge here?" Consciously, whoever is most self-denying and polite is the winner. Subconsciously, the competition is on.

The best way for both people to handle this is to keep relating through conscious Girlchild, while focusing their subconscious Boychild determination into causes that Girlchild delights in. If the two can truly care for each other and for a cause they embrace, instead of getting into a Boychild game of who cares more than whom, they will enjoy a thriving relationship and accomplish much good together.

Girl-Boy Meets Girl-Mother

Girl-Boys and Girl-Mothers get along well, because they are not aggressive with each other. Both consciously want to save the world, with their subconscious wisdom and action. Sometimes it can be difficult for them to communicate, because they are both spherical thinkers. If they are dining out together, for instance, they may find it necessary to reel the waiter into their conversation so they can feel the safety of a grounding presence.

Generally, Girl-Boys dominate the relationship and Girl-Mothers serve as a strong backup for them. Girl-Boys' subconscious Boychild ends up directing their initiative and Girl-Mothers' subconscious Mother supplies him with the "who, what, where, when and why" coordinates he needs to succeed.

If any conflict occurs, it would start in the subconscious, and not be clear who is to blame. The two may become hostile, either because Girl-Mothers' subconscious Mother abandoned Girl-Boys' subconscious Boychild or because subconscious Boychild turned aggressive on Girl-Mothers' conscious Girlchild.

Consciously, the two may be completely oblivious to what is going on. They may be relating to each other with the biggest of smiles and the best of intentions, never realizing that serious subconscious issues are eroding their relationship.

This problem can be overcome if the two will refrain from engaging in Unloved Girlchild victim behavior and truly care for each other through their Loved Girchild. Then, with the help of their subconscious Mother and Boychild abilities, they will create a dynamic partnership.

Girl-Boy Meets Girl-Father

When Girl-Boys and Girl-Fathers come together, Girl-Fathers quickly establish their line of authority through subconscious Father and Girl-Boys go along with it. They both want to change the world, and agree that having Girlchild at the conscious level poses a challenge. Subconsciously, Girl-Fathers can create the right matrix for success, and Girl-Boys can help them carry out their plans.

Problems may arise if Girl-Fathers' internal criticism pattern starts leaking out, and Girl-Boys pick it up and respond aggressively. Then, Girl-Fathers may blame their Girlchild for having made friends with an aggressive person, and unleash Unloving Father's criticism onto everybody.

If both people can tone down their Unloved Girlchild's hypersensitivity to perceived malintent, the relationship will prosper, especially if they tie themselves to a cause greater than themselves.

Girl-Mother Meets Girl-Mother

Girl-Mothers get along fine with each other, because conscious Girlchildren tend to enjoy each other's company. They have no animosity, only the potential for mutual aloofness. In this case, if one Girlchild were to feel slighted by the other person's subconscious aloofness and be up front about it, the other Girlchild would most likely apologize.

The irony of this relationship is that unless both people have a reason for staying together outside of themselves, they tend to go their separate ways, because there is no dynamic tension between them. The exception to this is if they have a common cause that gives them a goal to work towards. Then, their innate intuition and adult competency can go far in creating a highly creative and emotionally stable union.

Girl-Mother Meets Girl-Father

Girl-Mothers and Girl-Fathers tend to be a good match. Both people have a conscious desire to take care of the world, and their conscious Girlchildren get along well. Subconsciously, they are very adult with each other and use their maturity to guide them.

When the two get together, Girl-Mothers usually defer to Girl-Fathers. Subconscious Father likes to give marching orders. Then, subconscious Mother analyzes the situation and makes it work. Finally, conscious Girlchild tries to deliver the goods.

Problems only arise if Girl-Fathers' subconscious criticism of their own conscious Girlchild is picked up by Girl-Mothers. Then, Girl-Mothers may react defensively and stop following Girl-Fathers' subconscious Father agenda. Girl-Fathers' Unloving Father would interpret this as mutiny and the relationship would break down.

To work things out, it is key for both people to establish healthy Loving Father boundaries. When their Loving Father is active, Girl-Fathers can stop assessing others through their own subconscious criticism, and Girl-Mothers can stop allowing others to define them. By establishing Loving Father boundaries, both people can feel safe and self-confident with each other and with other people, and bring out the best in each other.

Girl-Father Meets Girl-Father

If Girl-Fathers meet themselves in another person, the two get along fine, unless their internal criticism gets the best of them. If one conscious Girlchild starts to pick up criticism from the other Girl-Father, they may get edgy. The relationship may even end abruptly, because neither person wants the other person mirroring back to them their own worst trait—their subconscious Unloving Father criticism. If, however, one of the two can bring up the Loving Father at the conscious level to protect Girlchild, that sabotage can be thwarted.

What is especially nice about a relationship between two Girl-Fathers is that even when both people have a different way of doing things, they will honor what works for the other person and look for win-win solutions. They feel no need to compete over whose system is better, who is right or who is going to do the best job. It is precisely that ability to impersonally refrain from negative competition that is the secret of their individual and mutual success.

Show—Don't tell.

Infinite striving to be the best is man's duty;
it is its own reward.
Everything else is in God's hands.
—Mohandas Gandhi

You can be your best self no matter what archetypal pattern you have. When you consciously determine to claim the strength of your Loving Father, the wisdom of your Loving Mother, the action principle of your Loved Boychild and the inspiration of your Loved Girlchild, you become authentic. You are no longer boxed in by inherited, negative patterns of behavior. You can achieve your full potential.

Your striving for wholeness will impact the people in your life and ripple out to everyone you come into contact with. Time and time again, Caroline and Brian's clients have been surprised that as they worked with their inner family archetypes, the people they were involved with would also change, without any prompting. Caroline and Brian eventually called this "the watershed effect."

A woman named Judy started coming to Caroline and Brian for counseling and worked very hard on transcending her unloving archetypes. One day, she came for her weekly session and was in a panic. "My in-laws are coming and it is terrible," she said.

"What's wrong?" Caroline and Brian asked.

"I clean my house for a whole week and then my mother-in-law comes in and goes straight to the place that I missed. It is like she's got a sonar. I've had it happen three or four times already."

"Let's just work the system," they told her. "Do a good sweep of your place. Then, ask one of your friends to come in and have a look."

"It doesn't matter," she said. "I've tried that."

"Then what we're going to do," they said, "is work on accepting the fact that your mother-in-law does not designate who you are. Your higher self designates who you are and you're not going to give that power to your mother-in-law anymore." Judy agreed.

Her in-laws arrived at the airport. They greeted each other with a stiff embrace and went directly to Bill and Judy's home. As soon as they got there, the mother in law went straight to the kitchen and "smelled something." Bill responded by immediately taking the garbage out. Then, while sitting at the dinner table, Bill's father started to tell one of his usual stories, the kind families like to tell over and over again.

"You know, Dad," said Bill, "I've heard that story a hundred times and have told it myself. But I was there and I remember that's not really what happened."

Bill's father blew up. "Who do you think you are telling me what happened? You were a kid." he said. "That's it. Margaret, pack our bags." And they were on a jet, going back across the continent. Judy's mother-in-law never had a chance to find the messy corner in the house.

A few weeks later, Judy came in for a counseling session and said, "You won't believe what happened. My mother-in-law phoned the other night and I picked up the phone. She asked me to put Bill on the phone, because his father wanted to talk to him.

" 'Hello, hello?' said Bill. 'Nobody's there.'

"Finally his father answered.

" 'Is that you, Bill?'

" 'Dad? What's up, Dad?'

"His father answered: 'Well, I just want you to know that my old man was a mean, old S.O.B. He would always kick me in the behind so I had to kick you in your behind. That's just the way we are and that's all.'

" 'What are you talking about, Dad?' said Bill.

"And his dad broke down in tears. Bill had never heard or seen his father cry.

" 'No, Dad, no, no. I'm sorry. Is this about the story?'

" 'Of course it is about the story. We have to tell that story. It is the only way that we can keep things right.'

" 'What things? What's going on here? Dad, we need to talk.'

" 'Yes, you're right. We're going to come and talk this out.' "

So, in the week that followed, Judy started to panic again that her mother-in-law was coming and that she had to clean the house.

"We met at the airport," she told Caroline and Brian. "We were standing there waiting for them. My father-in-law gave my husband a full-body hug. I could not believe it. You could see the tears flowing out of Bill's eyes over his father's shoulder. Then my mother-in-law came up and hugged me and held onto me longer than I held onto her." The housecleaning was no longer an issue.

This is one of many stories. People who work with their inner family archetypes have seen the watershed effect blessing their loved ones, over and over again.

Bill's parents may never know that the growth they experienced was a result of Judy's own transformation, which rubbed off on Bill and then on her in-laws.

Each new level of growth we achieve influences the people around us and gradually transforms every relationship we have. As we demonstrate *our* personal overcoming through our actions, the people in our lives will also begin to change. We do not have to mention anything and oftentimes, it is better if we don't.

Practicing the presence of the four loving archetypes makes us self-determined. We no longer allow others to define us. We no longer simply ride the roller coaster of life's ups and downs. We sit in the driver's seat. The power of self-transformation is in our hands. We take the barbs, the arrows and the jabs life throws at us with more dignity and dexterity, because we know these are tests that will lead us to greater self-mastery. We keep striving, we focus on what is in front of us, we are merciful with our shortfalls, and we do not give up.

Little by little, we find that we can succeed again and again. This makes us feel more competent, more confident and more in sync with life. We experience new levels of harmony and connectedness in our relationships with others. Self-transcendence is no longer someone else's experience or just a self-help theory. It is something we've earned. It is our own realization.

Bibliography

Aimee: Life Story of Aimee Semple McPherson. Foursquare Publications, Los Angeles, CA., 1979.

Coleridge, Samuel Taylor. *Poetical Works:* "Kubla Khan". Oxford University Press, 1974.

Crum, Tom. *The Magic of Conflict*. Prentice Hall, 1998

De Bertodano, Teresa ed. *Daily Readings with Mother Teresa*. Harper Collins, 1993

Gibran, Kahlil. *The Prophet*. New York, N.Y.: Knopf Publishing, 2000

Hay, Louise. *You Can Heal Your Life*. Hay House Inc., 1995

Hill, Napoleon. *Think and Grow Rich*. Fawcett Publications, Inc., Greenwich, CT., 1960

Jung, C.G.. *The archetypes and the collective unconscious* (R.F.C. Hull, Trans.): Princeton University Press, 1969

The King James Bible

McKay, Hill and Buckler: *A History of Western Society*. Third Edition. Houghton Mifflin Co., 1987.

Paramahansa Yogananda, *Inner Reflections 2000*. Self Realization Fellowship, 2000.

Powers, Margaret Fishback. *Footprints*. New York, N.Y.: Walker and Company, 1998.

Pressfield, Steven. *The War of Art: Winning the Inner Creative Battle*. New York, N.Y.: Rugged Land, 2002

Prophet, Mark and Elizabeth Clare. *The Great White Brotherhood in the Culture, History and Religion of America*. Summit University Press,1975

-- -- --*The Science of the Spoken Word*, Summit University Press, 1991

Randall, Willard Sterne. *George Washington, A Life*. Henry Holt and Company, NY., 1997

Redfield, James.*The Celestine Prophecy: An Adventure*. Warner Books, 1995.

Reiss, Haydn. *Rumi: Poet of the Heart*. Magnolia Films, 1999

Silverman, Lloyd; Lachmann, Frank; Milich, Robert. *The Search for Oneness*. New York, N.Y.: International Universities Press, Inc., 1982.

For more information,

please visit us at

www.innerfamilyarchetypes.com.

Find out about:

- ◆ scheduling a personal consultation

- ◆ other products

- ◆ hosting a seminar or a workshop in your area

- ◆ corporate and facilitator training

You can also contact The Sirius Consulting Group

In the United States at:

The Sirius Consulting Group
PO Box 5145
Bozeman, MT 59718
USA

In Canada at:

The Sirius Consulting Company
1430 6A St. N.W.
Calgary, AB, Canada
T2M 3G7

About the authors

Caroline Hanstke, and Brian and Therese Emmanuel Grey

Caroline Hanstke has served as a psychologist in the public and private sectors for more than thirty-five years, with extensive counseling, teaching, management and human resource experience. She runs a counseling practice in Calgary, Canada, and is a member of the College of Alberta Psychologists.

Brian Emmanuel Grey is an intuitive with an extensive focus on transformative psychology and on the practical application of Eastern and Western spiritual principles. He runs a private consulting practice in Bozeman, Montana.

In 1990, Caroline and Brian founded The Sirius Consulting Company in Calgary, Canada, to help people and businesses succeed. Since that time, they have worked with hundreds of individuals and businesses, including multinational companies and government agencies. They have applied the inner family archetype model to effect positive changes in the workplace and to foster genuine growth in personal relationships. They have also delivered the information presented in this book in seminars, corporate training workshops and to clients around the world.

Therese Emmanuel Grey is a journalist who has written about personal growth for more than a decade. She first started working with the inner family archetypes as a client and personally experienced their transforming power in her life. Today, she facilitates the inner family archetype model in workshops, seminars and publications.

In 2004, Caroline, Brian and Therese founded The Sirius Consulting Group and Sirius Publishing Partners in the United States to publish and promote tools for self-transcendence. For more information, please visit www.innerfamilyarchetypes.com.

Use These Coupons!

Not sure about your archetypes?

Only $20

for an initial archetypal assessment

Call 1-877-WHYWEDO to make an appointment.

Learn more about how your personal archetypes affect your relationships.

$15 off

a follow-up $75 archetypal consultation

Call 1-877-WHYWEDO to make an appointment.